Girly Stories
Significant Moments of a Woman's Life

By
Chelsea Brewer

I dedicate this book to every woman
I have ever known.
These are our stories,
yours and mine.

But mostly I dedicate this to my soul mate,
my other half,
my mother,
Laurie.

Girly Stories

The_____Moment of a Woman's Life

Have to get in there and do this. Can't be scared. Just do it and get it over with. Fuck the groceries. Didn't even need them. Just leave them there and you'll put them away later. Man I have to pee. Quick, get in there. You don't need your purse. Leave your purse outside. You don't need your keys; leave your keys with your purse. Idiot.

That's what got you into this mess. You're an idiot. Look, you even locked the door behind you. No one else lives here. Who's going to walk in? Stupid. Okay, just do this. Okay, *how* do I do this?

Open the box. I'm sure there are directions inside. No, no, where are they? Oh, maybe they're inside this wrapper with it. Rip it open. Just rip it open. Okay, there they are. Man, this thing doesn't look so hard. You can do this. You've done it before, so long ago though.

Okay, just breathe. Relax. Maybe if I sit down for a sec. There you go. Okay, slowly. Now take off the cap. Put it down. You have to stand up real quick. Get those pants off. Stupid belt. Where were you that night? Shut up, get this done. Now, you got to hold this thing down there. Well, first you have to lift up the lid you idiot. Jesus Christ, you are so stupid. How have you survived this long?!

All right. Sit down, deep inhale, and exhale. Here we go, one, two, three, peeeeee..... Just enough to get it nice and wet. Ha ha. Nice and wet it was. Shut up. See, this isn't so hard. Man, thank God no one else lives here because you wouldn't want them walking in on you right now. You look like you're masturbating while you're peeing. That's one fetish that you wouldn't want anyone to know about. Okay, that should be enough. Put that handy dandy cap on. Shit, I just pissed all over my hand. That's great. Really great, and attractive, too. What am I worrying about being attractive for? I'm about to gain a ton of weight for one night of passion. You are such an idiot. Okay, pants back on. Fuck, wipe your hand off first. Poor towel, you never deserved this fate.

Okay. Pants are back on. It says to leave it on a flat surface. Aaaaaaannnddddd, for five minutes. Okay, all right, what do I do for five minutes? I'll go put those groceries away. Shit! You knocked it over, stupid!! Quick, put it back! Just put it back and leave it there. Now back away. Leave the room before you blow it up or something.

I'm so scared. Why are you scared? Why am I scared? This is the scariest thing anyone can go through. Whether you want it to happen or not. What will I do? How will I get through this? How will I explain fifteen years from now how I just wanted a quick lay with an old friend? Old friend, indeed. My dearest, this "old friend" hadn't called you in four years prior and hasn't called you since. This was a mistake. It was all a huge mistake. Lettuce goes in crisper drawer.

But what if it wasn't a mistake? What if I'm meant to do this? What if this is how it's supposed to happen? Everything happens for a reason, right? What if this is supposed to happen right now in my life when: A. I least expect it and/or B. when I least want it? That's how everything happens. Winning the lottery, death, rape, finding out a kid you went to school with is a pro-football player now. All unplanned events. You can't really plan anything, it all just happens. Crackers on top shelf.

Okay, okay fine. I can accept that things just happen. But you don't want this. You don't want a friggin' baby. You're not ready to be a mother. But I might not have a choice. What are you talking about? You have a choice, it's known as pro-choice. Oh God, I couldn't go through with it. Why not? It's not illegal, it's not wrong. It's an option. I can't. I can't go through with any of this. I wish I were dead. I wish I could start over. Be born again and start over and learn from this mistake and never make it again and wait until I was married to have sex and everything would be okay. La la land is so beautiful. Scotch tape on desk.

Well, what do you want me to think? I can't handle this. I'm not ready for a kid. I'm not ready for the responsibility. I'm not ready for any of this. I can't be in charge of another person's life. Look at how I fuck up my own. No, no I can't do this. I can't do this. How could I possibly do this? No child could ever benefit from belonging to me. No child could ever possibly make it if it was under my care and supervision. I could never make it with a child. Is it so bad really, to not want a child? Is it so bad to want to put my career, my life, *myself* first? Don't I want to be good, centered, balanced, rid of all the ghosts? Capable and independent and prepared for all the crazy things life can throw at me? I can't even afford a nice pair of boots. How can I take care of a child? Oh God, oh God. I'm gonna throw up, I'm gonna throw up. Oh God, I need to sit down. Lie down. This kitchen floor is so cold. Put the cold against your skin. Just breathe. It'll be okay, sweetie. It'll be okay, breathe. Just breathe.

It's time.

Must get up. Slowly now. Push body up. Grab edge of counter, pull up. Stand. Wait, wait.....wait. Walk slowly. Don't close your eyes. You'll faint and never know.

Okay. There it is.

And there *it* is.

There she is. Or he.

Heritage

She wasn't the first one in her family to have cancer. Her mother had it years ago. Both of her mother's parents had died from it. Her mother's sister had had it not too long ago. And more recently, that sister's husband was dying from it.

When she found the lump, her brow furrowed. Concern washed over her fingertips as they felt it again, and her stomach dropped. For a moment, she panicked. There on the brown carpet of her bedroom floor, half naked and in the middle of the night, she panicked. He heart sped up, her breath quickened, and her eyes opened wide. She felt it again, and for the first time in her life, she prayed to God to not let her die.

By now, she couldn't remember if she had told her mother or the doctor first. She had blanked out about everything and could only see the lump itself pulsate in the darkness of dense tissue in her left breast. She could look at her naked breast and see it sticking out right next to her nipple. There it was, plain as day: the beginning of the end.

Of course, she *couldn't* see it on the outside. And frankly, on the inside it was about the size of a bee-bee. But for a twenty-year-old girl, it could have been a fucking watermelon. It didn't make a difference how big it was. It was there. In an otherwise perfectly healthy budding young woman, it was there.

During the few days she had to wait to see the doctor, she didn't talk much. Her mother had told her father and brother. They remained silent yet strong around her; invisible support where she didn't need to talk about it to make her feel better. She attached herself to her mother. She lay in bed next to her; she went with her to the store. She was two years old again, anxious for the comfort only a mommy could give. Her best friend tried to talk to her, actually said that if there was anything she could do to simply name it. She only shouted at her just to leave her alone, that all she wanted was her mother and for the whole thing to not really be happening.

She would lay in bed with her mother, fall asleep to the TV and dream about what would happen to her. She would lose some weight. Well, that wasn't too bad. But she would lose some hair, too. She would shave it all off before it could fall out, just like her aunt had done. One fell swoop instead of the torturous morning after morning of waking up to chunks of it on her pillowcase. But she wouldn't wear a wig like her aunt had. She could never stand wigs on her head. She'd have to wear a cap or a turban. They'd have to do a mastectomy, like her grandmother. And she would walk in all of the breast cancer walks with her one breast and be as proud as she could be. Or she could slowly and painfully die, like her uncle was doing now.

The doctor ordered an ultrasound, of course. She had expected that. But for whatever reason, this scared her even more. It made it more serious, more real, more out of control and unpredictable, more powerful than her. She had never had an ultrasound before and even though the ultrasound tech tried to warm up the sticky goo, it was still cold on her bare skin. She watched the screen, desperately looking for it, wanting to see it in all of its glory. She asked the tech questions just to comfort her own mind. The tech conveyed a little humanity by showing her where her spleen and other organs were. In her head she imagined what it would be like to see a little baby up on the screen. A figure of gray matter with eyes, fingers and toes all ready to be kissed repeatedly by family members. What a trip it would be to see something like that up there, knowing it was inside of her. Inside of her. Her mind suddenly found its way back to the lump.

They told her it would be about two days and

they would let her know. She quit smoking then and there figuring that was what had gotten her here in the first place. She started back up the next day due to simple stress and frustration and also because she figured she would die anyway. Speed it up a notch. She was a very patient person. But the thought of literally rotting away made her so angry... She smoked two packs that second day.

The ultrasound came back with the result of "nothing turned up." She scheduled a second opinion right away but had to wait two more days. She fell into a spell of scattered attacks of insomnia. Dreams of huge black and red spiders with webs in every corner of her house that she was constantly walking into or swimming in a lake filled with sharks with no shore to climb onto. She did not attend any classes; she did not return any phone calls. Her family talked in hushed voices when she was out of the room for fear of upsetting her. Her mother offered to go with her to the second opinion meeting, but she said no. She might as well face it herself.

She lay and waited in the God-awful mauve room in a hospital gown that was too small, for a man that was not her regular doctor to come in and tell her she was dying and that there was no hope. A mastectomy could be performed but it had probably already spread to her bones and blood and brain. She would slowly go insane and lose all control of her bodily functions and would have to remain in a hospice since she only had a matter of months to live. She may as well start a will and give her petty belongings to all of her friends and keep the nice things for her family. And all she would be able to see would be darkness, darkness, darkness. The door opened and the doctor walked in.

The nurse observed as the doctor felt his way around to the lump. He hummed and hawed for a moment. Then as simply as he could possibly say it, "Fibrocystic." She blinked. "Group of hormones." She inhaled. "Very common for your age group." She parted her lips. "Nothing to worry about." She exhaled. "It will go away in time." She smiled.

And that was that. All her worry melted and evaporated into the air. Her fear, her anxiety, the songs to be played at her funeral all disappeared and she smiled again. She thanked him for an answer and for all of his help. He smiled right back and handed her several pamphlets. The nurse smiled as she continued her observation, and they left the room so she could get dressed. She got off the table and looked in the mirror on the wall and smiled again. The world had changed; everything was different.

In her car, she donned her sunglasses and blared David Bowie. She swooped her hand up and down in the contrasting wind outside her window. She drove faster than she should have but didn't care, a ticket couldn't get her down. Nothing could ever get her down ever again. Her mother cried and hugged her when she told her the wonderful news. Her father and brother again were silent but smiled. A weight was lifted, a curse was ended. She had broken the chain and was going to live. All of her dreams were right in front of her and she wanted them as if they were oxygen and she had been held underwater.

Her body was hers again, and it was fresh and

pink and healthy and beautiful. She bought herself a new purple bra to celebrate the beauty of her breasts. She slept with it on that night and dreamt of everything she could possibly be: a mother, a teacher, a secret agent. She saved the world and won an Oscar. She received the Pulitzer Prize and built a skyscraper. She ran a hundred miles and never stopped singing.

False Security

Elaina sat in the corner like a disobedient catholic schoolgirl. Only this time she was thirty years old instead of thirteen, and she was there not because she had passed a note or giggled out of context, but because she had mopped herself there without even realizing it until it was too late.

She had used one of those new environmentally friendly wood-floor polishing oils. She used it once before in the hallway - a small section in case it didn't work. But it worked great, and she was incredibly pleased with the shine and the lovely orange scent in the hallway. Her only qualm with it was it took almost a half hour to dry. She had to keep the kids outside until it did, otherwise they would ruin the lovely woodsy grove Elaina pictured growing in her hallway.

Now she was stuck on a chair in the far corner of her living room with a half hour to kill. She felt like an absolute moron.

The kids, Mark and Molly, were at pre-school, which is why she chose this time to mop. Since it would take so long to dry, she needn't worry about unnecessary traffic in the main room of the house. Her husband, John, was at work. He had a home security business. All day long he would tell people how their lives were in danger, even in the comfort of their own homes, and how they should never trust anyone that knocks on their front door, not even when it's him coming to install their system. He could be quite scary and unnerving at times.

Elaina planned on cleaning up the kitchen while the floor dried. The rest of the family left their breakfast dishes and glasses on the table just like every other day. She was going to wash all the dishes, scrub the stove, and clean out the fridge. That should take about a half hour. Then she would be free to walk on the gleaming scented floors of the living room and into her bedroom where she would have her weekly cry and take a short nap.

The crying had become a routine event about three months ago when it officially hit Elaina that she had let herself go. Not only physically; she *had* gained about fifty pounds that she hadn't been able to shed since having her first child five years ago. She had let her life go, her dreams and her spirit had slipped through her fingers. She had become a person that she never thought she could become. It wasn't being a wife or mother that bothered her. It was *only* being a wife and mother that killed her.

15

John didn't seem to mind that Elaina wanted to continue working through her pregnancy when she was expecting Mark. He was impressed that she felt energized enough to keep going. She was head of Human Resources for Sweet Water Investment Services. Even though she sat at a desk all day, denying and approving forms, reading complaints and concerns, it was a highly stressful position. But Elaina had no interest in letting pregnancy slow her down, it just wasn't her style.

She worked right up until she hit thirty-nine weeks. She made it all the way through that final week without going into labor and everybody there surprised her on her last Friday by invading her office with balloons and flowers, all of them singing "Isn't She Lovely" at the top of their lungs. She laughed so hard at their hilarious gesture that she did, in fact, pee a little in her slacks. It was impossible not to, being that far along and laughing that hard.

She went into labor two days later and it was a breeze. Twelve hours total from first contraction to final push. Elaina's doctor was happy and joked that he hardly even needed to be there and she should bill herself. Now *that* was her style: independent and efficient.

Like so many other mommies when they hold their first newborn, Elaina decided that she would not be going back to work and would be a full-time stay-at-home mom. Of course, everybody humored her and figured she'd snap out of it by month two, three at the latest. 'Elaina is too independent for that,' everyone whispered, 'There's no way she's going to last at home all day. No way!'

It actually took until the end of month five when she started getting cabin fever and craved for adult conversations and cocktail hour. The longer she stayed home, the more she realized how much she wanted to go back to school to become a teacher. Elaina had always wanted to teach and got a head start years ago, but took an extended break after getting her job at Sweet Water. The money was good. The fact that she didn't have homework everyday was better. She met John a few weeks after getting the job, and they married a year later. When Elaina got pregnant on their honeymoon, she was too excited to even think about anything else.

When Mark turned six months, Elaina approached John with the notion of her going back to school instead of work. He was not keen to the idea. "Who's going to watch the baby while you're in class?" he asked. "They have a daycare there at the college. It'd be perfect!" she excitedly reported. He shrugged and looked away. When he looked back at her, he shook his head. "I don't know, Babe, those places are employed by other students who are just trying to get work credits. I don't trust them with our new baby."

Elaina looked into five other daycares, from the lady next door to a fancy baby day-resort. John had rejected them all for various reasons. "Maybe when the baby is older, when he can walk around and understand a few things, then you can go back to school," he told her. And so it began: the man of the house had spoken, and the woman of the house obeyed.

Right after Mark's first birthday, Elaina

brought the subject up again, and again John rejected it, still uncomfortable with some stranger watching their child. All of their family members that lived in town worked full time and wouldn't be able to take care of little Mark. So he suggested that she wait until Mark got into pre-school to start taking classes. Once again, she obeyed.

Only one month later, Elaina discovered she was pregnant again with Molly and for the next three years, she juggled pregnancy, then two growing children, and keeping their household. All the while, John was getting more and more irritable with each passing day. He would get home from work and would want "alone time" to go into the computer room and play his shoot 'em up games with the baby gate up so nobody could bother him. And God help her if dinner wasn't ready within a half hour of him getting home; that would just make his terrible day worse. "I work so hard all damn day, all I want is to come home, unwind, have a good meal and relax. Why is that so hard for you to grasp?" he would say.

Elaina started keeping her opinions to herself just so he wouldn't get any angrier. For all she knew, work *was* awful, business was awful, and not enough people needed security systems. John never told her what was going on during the day that made him so miserable at night. They stopped having sex. Once every two or three months John would reach out for her breast and give it a squeeze, raising his eyebrows. Elaina gave in every time, thinking that she had to since they were married, even though she never got any enjoyment out of the eight to ten minutes of clumsy humping.

The last time she mentioned going back to school, John threw a fit like a child. "What the fuck are you talking about? You can't go back to school! You have a family to take care of. Who's supposed to take care of the house while you're in class all fucking day?!? I am NOT hiring a fucking maid, I am NOT made of money, Elaina!"

They had a semi-blowout about it. It wasn't full blown just because she had adapted to his irrational temper and knew not to yell too much or push too hard or he would really get angry. Once, and only once, he hurt her. He grabbed her by both arms and held her up to him and shouted into her face, leaving fingertip sized bruises on her triceps. Elaina had to wear long sleeve shirts for over a week when that happened.

School would have to wait until the kids themselves were in school all day. John told her she could take an online class or two, that way she could slowly work towards her degree, "But still keep your attention on what's really important: this family of ours," he said. Elaina scoffed at the online classes. She took one class and dropped it after two months because the tests never seemed to match up to the notes given in the lectures.

Elaina surrendered to her new life: wife, mother, and housekeeper. All day she would watch their kids, clean up messes, change diapers, play cartoon DVDs, make breakfast, lunch and dinner for the lot of them, and squeeze a shower in during the hour nap the kids would take in the late afternoon.

She had no idea what had happened to her. She was the girl who was going to do everything.

Travel to Europe every few years, write a novel, teach high school dropouts to read and write, better her life so she could help others better theirs. Somehow her husband had become someone she didn't know. John had turned into Dr. Frankenstein, and she his misshapen monster that he vehemently loathed.

Elaina sat in the corner and looked over at the clock sitting on the mantel. She had to lean forward to see it and almost fell out of the chair onto the moist shiny floor. She caught herself just as she saw ten minutes had passed. Twenty more to go.

When it hit her three months ago that she had let her life go, she was in her bedroom getting dressed after a shower. She glanced at herself in the mirror and was struck by what she saw: a puffy, pasty and dimpled version of herself. Elaina had seen herself in this full-length mirrored closet door a thousand times, but that day, she saw herself *exactly* as she now was as if it were the first time she'd seen herself ever.

She stopped clasping her bra and froze there, her elbows pointing outwards, perusing her reflection for a moment. She unhooked her bra and tossed it onto the bed behind her. Then she took off her panties and tossed them next to the bra, turned and stood facing the mirror, and stared at her nude figure. Her arms were flat and squishy now, not toned and shapely like they were six years ago. Her breasts hung low like two half-empty bags of bread. Her belly pushed out above her swollen hips as if she were five months pregnant again. Her thighs clung together like two sisters holding on for dear life. They used to have three perfect diamonds between them, showcasing her hard work in daily runs and weekend Pilates sessions. Even her feet had changed, now square and wide, like men's feet.

Elaina barely recognized herself; even her own face had plumped over her sharp cheekbones and sleek jaw-line. She no longer resembled the sexy and radiant young woman she knew. Her marriage had been a cocoon, but instead of a butterfly, she had emerged a pale and doughy mother of two, spending her days making beds and grocery shopping, filling the void left behind from the nonexistence of her previous life.

It was in that moment that her world fell apart. Elaina had completely metamorphosed without any realization of its taking place. Standing there in her bedroom, naked and vulnerable, hating the reflection of the woman in front of her, she started crying. She stood there bawling and watched her body. She watched the thick belly and pendulous breasts heave. She watched her chubby form quake and jiggle with each violent sob. The more she cried, the more her body vibrated. The more her body vibrated, the more she cried. And there in her bedroom, her weekly routine began of hating herself for who she had become and for letting herself get there.

She would get Mark and Molly ready in the morning while John drank his coffee and ate his egg whites with dill and pepper she had specially prepared for him. He would read the paper and scratch himself and clear his throat while she struggled to get Molly into her corduroy pants and argue with Mark about taking another backpack with him to school filled with all of his Spiderman toys. Then he would disappear into the bathroom just as she was snapping the kids into their car seats and stopping them in the middle of their morning slap fight.

After dropping them off at school, she would make her way back to the empty house (John never waited for her to get back to say goodbye for the day even though he left about two minutes before she got home) and clean all the dishes from the three of them (since John never did the dishes before he left), eat whatever cold eggs or soggy cereal was leftover, go into her bedroom and have a good, loud cry. She would let it all out for about an hour or so. Sometimes she was surprised at how guttural she sounded and how the neighbors never seemed to hear her and come check to see if things were okay. Maybe they didn't want to embarrass her, maybe they didn't care, or maybe they couldn't even hear her. It didn't matter. Elaina took this time for herself to emotionally bleed. It was a wound that always hurt and never healed, and she couldn't stop picking at the sutures.

It's not as though this routine made Elaina feel better every week. Almost every time she cried she felt worse that she still felt badly enough about herself to actually continue to have a weekly emotional breakdown. It felt amazing to cry, but awful to have to. This is why she kept it to once a week. Only once or twice a second cry had worked itself into her week and it sent her into a deep depression, keeping her numb and functional enough only to do her daily housewife tasks. She hardly spoke during this depression and John became wildly angry at her moodiness. The last few times another cry tried to creep itself in, Elaina kept it in check.

That was the only thing she had control of anymore. John had taken so much of her power away, that she didn't even have her name on their bank accounts. "If something happens on the account then I can handle it without it affecting you. It's safer this way. Besides, if you really need money just tell me what for and I'll give it to you," he told her.

It wasn't long after the first cry that Elaina realized the kind of controlling, possessive person John really was. Besides the bank accounts, her name wasn't on the deed to the house ("I'll will it to you and you'll just inherit it anyways."), or the cars ("You don't need your own car, it's less debt for you to worry about."), and he completely forbad her to get a part time job ("If you think I can't provide for this family, maybe you shouldn't be a part of it.").

She was trapped. He made it virtually impossible for her to leave. Just by saying "Yes Dear" all the time and "Whatever you say, Dear" she had helped in laying out the trap and knowingly stepped right into it.

The clock on the mantel told her ten more minutes had passed. Elaina toed the sheen on the floor in front of her: still tacky.

It was in these last three months of Elaina breaking down and feeling what she had kept bottled up for so long, that she decided it was time to leave. And today was the big departure. Her plan had come

23

into fruition right after she bought the earth-friendly floor cleaner: save the planet and your own life with this bottle of organic cleaner! As she mopped her hallway that first afternoon, other than noticing the fantastic scent, she plotted her exit from this household. In two weeks time, Elaina would have a day like any other day. She would get up with the kids, make their breakfast, brush their teeth, and dress them. Then she would wake John up since alarms were "either not loud enough or too loud" to wake up to, make his breakfast and drive the kids to school. Then come home without so much as a thank you note or 'I LOVE YOU' written on the bathroom mirror in steam waiting for her. She would begin her chores: mop the floor, clean the kitchen, have her weekly cry for motivational purposes, take a nap, wake up, make the bed, and clean up the bathrooms. At that point she would normally go grocery shopping or pick up stuff for the house or John's dry cleaning. Instead, she would use this time to pack her things, and when she finished, pack up the kids.

She would finish in time to pick the kids up from school. Instead of driving to her mother's on the other side of town, she was going to drive to her friend Maren's house about a half hour away. John would surely go to her mother's whether or not she was actually there. There would be much less trouble if she wasn't.

Maren and Elaina had worked together at Sweet Water and became immediate friends. Elaina thought the world of her and trusted her with anything and everything. She was the only person Elaina ever complained to about John. When she told him she wanted to leave him, Maren gladly offered her house for shelter. Elaina contemplated it; it wasn't too far from the kids' school, they could still see their father, but there would be enough space between the two of them and she wouldn't have to worry about dealing with him showing up. He never liked Maren, and therefore never bothered to learn her whereabouts.

Elaina and the kids would hole up for a week or two while John's shock wore off. Then they would move in with her mother, and life would happen as it would, hopefully without too much drama. She never believed that John would react violently or crazy. He would definitely insist on getting full custody of the kids. She would have to fight him on that. She wasn't going to bother with anything else. He would take the house, cars, and money since it was all in his name anyway. All she wanted was to get away from him and this life she had succumbed to, with maybe a modest alimony.

The phone rang, startling Elaina out of her deep thought. She looked over at the kitchen phone and waited for the machine to pick up. After the beep: "Hey Honey, it's me. I don't know where the hell you could be right now, but whatever. Look, I'll be home in about a half hour. The power's out here at the shop. Whole damn block is out! They have no idea when it's coming back on so I'm just waiting for a couple more minutes to make sure the alarm is going to function on the generator. Make sure the house looks nice, I'm having a work associate come over to discuss some, uh… options…for us. Maybe get some lunch ready. This might take some time.

There's some paperwork we have to fill out and sign. Oh, the alarm's working. I'll be home soon. "

Click. Dial tone.

Elaina dropped her head. The alarms didn't run off the power grid, they ran off of a battery-operated system. That way burglars or murderers or rapists couldn't just cut the power. He was lying. On top of everything else, Elaina's name wasn't anywhere near the business accounts. He wasn't bringing over any associate; he was bringing over a lawyer. Son of a bitch, he beat her to it.

Even in her organized plot, her lousy husband had to muck it all up. No matter, she would just reorganize around him. She had gotten used to doing that. She had become an expert, really.

Elaina lifted her head off her chest and stood up from the chair. Her butt had fallen asleep and the gravity shift sent pins and needles down the back of her thighs. She took a deep breath in and smelled the lovely orange scent in the house. She exhaled loudly, pushing all the breath from her body in a low hum. With her right foot first, she walked away from her corner and made her way to the bedroom to start packing, leaving a faint trail of footsteps behind her in the shiny perfect floor.

Eulogy

How can he be gone? Wake up Daddy? I see you. I know you're going to wake up.

I'm going to wake up alone for the rest of my life. I will never feel him again.

I feel so lost Daddy. Please come and find me. Come and take me to the park or your office or out to lunch. Anywhere that you want to go as long as you come and find me.

You'll find me looking for you. And I'll know that you're not there. You're not in your chair or out on the patio. You're not taking a shower or taking a nap. But I don't think I can ever stop looking.

Stop looking at me like that, assholes. I lost my father, I'll cry when I feel like it. I don't need your fucking pity.

Pity me, poor me. She's lost her husband and she's got nowhere to go. Why didn't I see it sooner? Why wasn't I more forceful with you? I should've made you go to the doctor when you started feeling sick.

I didn't know you were feeling sick. Mom never told me. You never told me.

You never told me how much you loved me. You told me you loved me all the time but never how much. Now I'll never know.

I'll never know why you had to go. It isn't fair. Why would you just go like that? How does it make sense for you to just go like you did? It's inexplicable. Just to leave like that.

Leave like that then. Just go without saying goodbye. I said I'd be right back. But you couldn't wait for me to get back so you could say goodbye.

All these people here to say goodbye. They really loved you didn't they?

Didn't they know it would be an open casket? They cry like they've never seen a dead body before.

I've never seen a dead body of someone I loved before. This is hard. It's healing. Well, it hurts like hell. But I know it will help me heal.

Help me heal Oh Lord. Help me grieve this death and heal me of my eternal wound. I will never stop crying.

I can't start crying. If I do, I'll lose it. I don't want any of these people to see me lose it. I have to be brave, I have to be strong.

I have to be strong now. I have to accept this and move on. Don't I? What if I can't? What if I'm not ready?

I'm not ready to lose you. I'm too young to lose my father. I'm too young to have to go through the rest of this world without you.

Without you, life has no meaning.

What is the meaning of life anyway? We live, we die. No matter what we do in between the two, we're going to die. Whether it is painful or in our sleep, sudden or drawn out, we will all die. This will never change. Living in a world of death eternal.

Living in a world without you.

You are my sunshine.

The sunshine will not be as bright as it was when you were here.

When you were here we would laugh.

We didn't dance enough. You need to come back so we can dance just a little more.

You need to come back so you can see what a good girl you raised. So you can continue to see the woman I will become.

I will become lonely and hollow. Dancing alone inside of my head. Nothing means anything anymore.

Anything I could do to bring you back would be so easy to do if I only knew what it was. Please tell me and I'll do it. God, please tell me.

Please tell me, God, how am I supposed to live through this? I don't want to. I cannot be alone. Not without my husband.

One day, my husband will go too soon. And then perhaps, I will feel like she feels.

I wish I could feel like she feels. Nature takes a parent first. But not a young husband so prematurely. We had so much more time. Is she lucky? Am I?

Am I the only one who is here? Is this a dream? Wake yourself up. Wake yourself up and this will all be over.

This will all be over soon. Then I can go home and get back into bed and I won't eat or speak until you walk through the door and get under the covers with me. Then this will all make sense.

None of this makes sense. How could I suddenly be an orphan just like that? I'm not even thirty.

Thirty years gone. Thirty years more. Why you? Why me? Our marriage had a chance. Our love was difficult, I admit that. But it was so real.

This is surreal.

How can I ever love again?

This is for the rest of my life.

This is for the rest of my life.

You will never come back to me.

You will not be coming back to me.

What am I going to do? How can I take care of her by myself?

How can I take care of her all by myself? I'm not strong enough.

I don't know if I'm strong enough to handle it. With her moods and complaints…

Her complaints. Her moods. The drama is sometimes just too much.

She's so much to handle. I wouldn't even know where to begin.

How would I even begin to understand her now? Without you...

Maybe it's not that difficult. Maybe it's right in front of me.

Maybe I can do this. Maybe if I just try a little harder.

This will be harder than I've ever known. I guess – I guess I can hold her.

I can hold her. I can still hold my baby. Our baby.

Just reach out, help me to reach out.

Help me to reach out to our baby.

.....

.....

Warm and familiar, soft and sweet. Mommy, why did God take Daddy away?

God had to take Daddy away, Baby. But Mommy's here. We must be here together.

I miss him.

We will miss him together.

The Fantasy of "Push"

"Come on, Love, it's time to go."

I rub my belly, glance across the street like I'm searching for meaning in life. I get in the car and take one last look at our house. This is the last time it will be just the two of us at this house. I get a pain in my heart so bad, it almost makes me cry as we pull out of the driveway.

The pregnancy has been good. No difficulties, no nausea, hardly any cravings even. Every check-up on time, every heartbeat loud and clear. Everything has been cool and calm. It's a pity my hips didn't spread, though. The calm waters are about to become choppy.

The drive seems longer than it actually is. We don't say much in the car. I sip my water and try to breathe normally. My nerves are boiling underneath the surface of my skin. I just know that any minute I'm going to lose it. I'll scream at the top of my lungs. I'll double over and projectile vomit. I'll open the car door and dive out, ready for the adrenaline rush that will meet me on the hot concrete.

My husband taps his index finger on the steering wheel to the beat of the music on the radio. Just taps his finger, no humming, no lip-syncing, nothing else, just tapping. It's his way of trying to find normalcy in an otherwise stressful situation. Then, he burps. I have to smile at his honesty. My hand goes to my belly again and I'm happy it's *his* child that I'm carrying.

We arrive at the hospital. As we're waiting in the left turn lane, I listen to the clicking blinker. It's like a time bomb linked to my fate. I'm scared to death that I'm going to die no matter what. I have the sudden urge to place my hand on my husband's and tell him to just keep going, like Thelma and Louise. No responsibilities, no obligations, just drive to freedom because I know it's there, just over the cliff. But no, my cowardice wins again and I say nothing. My husband turns into the parking lot and my stomach turns upside down. I'm terrified.

We gather everything together: my bag, his bag, the baby's bag, the camera bag, two pillows and my favorite blanket, a quilt my mother made me about two years ago. If it gets cold in there, no other blanket's warmth will comfort me. I'll be here for a few days and I must be comfortable. He shuts the door. "Have we got everything?" I kiss him softly, and we're ready to go.

I start zoning out. I notice the fountain by the sliding doors. I notice the elderly woman behind the front counter answering phones. She looks too old to be working. Briefly I contemplate whether I'll have to work that late in life, and if I do, will it be to make ends meet or just because I'm lonely? I answer every question at the check-in but I'm not really there. I sign what I have to sign but I'm gone. I see my hand move but I'm not attached to it. They escort us to our room and we try to make it home. We unpack a few things, I put on some socks. My husband's not saying much so I turn on the TV to ease the awkward silence but it has no sound. We have no choice now but to talk each other through this.

The words "common procedure," "no big deal" and "could've been worse" recycle themselves from our mouths over and over again. It'll all be worth it when it's over. But I can't help but to be terrified that this is the first time a scalpel will cut into my body. I've never been sliced before. I call myself a ham to ease my fear and make me laugh. But it only scares me more by giving me a visual of myself on the dinner table with pineapple slices atop my nipples. I shake the image from my head and pray it doesn't return.

A nurse finally shows to take my temperature, check my pulse, and strap me into the baby heart monitor. I put on my gown and I'm embarrassed that it doesn't close in the back. The most important day of my life and my ass is hanging out for everyone to see. I lie down as she gets the IV ready. I've never had one before. My husband takes my other hand and the nurse inserts the needle. I grip my husband's hand and want to yell "FUCK!" but I can't. It wouldn't be appropriate in front of the nurse or for the entire maternity ward. It's in and my mood has fallen. I'm officially ready to go home.

My frustration level is peaking. The nurse shaves my belly. She shaves off most of my pubic hair too. As the cool air hits my wet skin, my mood relaxes. Goosebumps give my body a tingling sensation and my shoulders loosen. I look at my almost hairless vagina and smile. I wonder if my husband will like it. A barrage of fantasies enter my brain of things we can do when we get home and one by one, they each end abruptly due to a screaming baby in the background. Damn these pregnancy hormones.

The nurse hands my husband his scrubs. We make some Lord of the Rings jokes about the paper hat. We say he's a gay orc or a fashionable fairy, things like that. He goes into the bathroom to change and I start to miss him once the door closes behind him. I'm scared he may never return and I'll have to deal with all of this reality all by myself. The nurse informs me that she's going to put my catheter in while my husband gets ready and I quietly shudder as my aforementioned fear is realized.

The catheter takes only a few minutes but it feels like at least an hour. It is the most intruded that my body has ever felt. I think of Frida Kahlo. I think of Jesus Christ. I think that I can't take much more of this or I'm going to punch the nurse in the goddamn throat and take off like a fucking madwoman being tested on against her will. She snaps off her gloves and pats my right thigh while announcing it's all over. I sigh relief, and start to cry just a little. My husband exits the restroom in full scrub garb and my spirits raise enough to give me a giggle. I comment on how cute he looks, how he'd make a good doctor. For a moment it's just him and me again. Then my family begins entering the room. I'm suddenly well aware of all of my pain and start to feel woozy.

The nurse puts a shower cap on my head. I can't seem to open my eyes. Maybe it's the IV. Maybe I'm about to pass out. Maybe I'm only dreaming. I become aware of and incredibly annoyed by the voices of my sister, mother, and father, all of my friends that have accompanied them here. I just want to go to sleep and let this all be over. I shouldn't be scared. I'm just having a baby. My father rubs my head over and over. My mother remains at the foot of the bed asking me how I'm doing and I only want to tell her that I'm hurting. My sister proudly states how she wasn't in so much pain when she went through *her* c-section prep and I shouldn't be so dramatic. My husband explains how I haven't had my epidural yet and before he can finish, my sister goes insane with wild disbelief and declarations on the shitty care that I'm receiving. Her anxiety passes to my feet and travels through my body like electricity. I open my eyes and give my husband a look that he knows very well. He asks the nurse how much longer and she says, "Not long." He looks back at me with an 'almost there' look. I just close my eyes again.

My patience is about to wear out with constant questions from everyone in there about how I feel, am I excited, et cetera. Finally the nurse asks everyone to leave since the doctor will be here soon. Each one kisses me goodbye, wishes me luck and shakes my husband's hand. As each one shuffles out, I remember one by one how I told them I was pregnant. The moments flash in my head and suddenly it's just me, my husband, the nurse and my unborn child. I suddenly cannot wait to hold my baby for the first time.

Moments later, the anesthesiologist comes in and introduces himself. Two nurses accompany him and hang behind him like gangsters, waiting to do his bidding. He tells me how they're going to take me to get my spinal now and the thugs get on either side of my bed. I sit up and slowly put my legs on the floor, trying not to disturb my lovely catheter. My nurse detaches the monitor plugs as I stand and I can no longer hear my child's heartbeat. I step off the bed and one of the thugs takes my hand to help me walk. The other takes the back of my gown to hold it together. In my modesty, I silently thank God for bringing the thug to my ass's rescue. I kiss my husband as they lead me out of the room and toward my new fate of motherhood. Will he be there when I wake up?

Everything is a dream now. I stumble down the hallway to another room completely bathed in white. They sit me on the edge of another bed and tell me to lean forward as far as I can. I take a few breaths and lean forward, my bulging belly about to slip into my mouth. I feel a terrible sting in the small of my back and cry out. The anesthesiologist says something: no good, one more time. I lean forward again. The anesthesiologist tries to coach me into leaning further but I can't. My child crowds inside of my belly. I hold my breath, clench my eyes, my fists and every other part of my body and lean over as far as I can. Another prick. I'm going to explode, then – it's in. I exhale. Whatever is happening now, I know I will not remember.

Things start getting misty, blurry. I hear my nurse say 'it's time.' I feel the thugs grab my hands and feet. They're tying me up to put me in the trunk of their car. I swim with the fishes tonight. I hear a squeaky wheel. Bright lights all around me. I'm in another room. All is black, then gray. A gray fog that doesn't smell like anything and isn't cold. I feel my back tingle. "Hello!" I'm lying down. I feel my husband's presence. He's at my shoulders, lightly rubbing them. "Count to ten!" Is it almost over? "Your baby's here!" Whoopity doo. Can I sleep now?

Vanscrashingchildrencryingmyweddingdaygreengras sthoselittlepinkflowersontreesinspringicanseemyfavo rilespotandhereismyfavoritesongwhichwaydidmymo thergocanihaveanotherchanceoreopancakeseltonjohni ssoniceforagaymankeeprunningcantmovetoofastwont getthereintimeitsjustlikefloatingfloatingfloatingwhoist hatcomingthisway?

"Love? Are you awake?"
My husband whispers as he caresses my hand.

Cold touches my face. I must be dead. It's all over. I am dead and always have been. So hungry for being dead. Why does my stomach hurt so much? I'm starving. I'm empty inside. I am a shell. Only scuffling sounds and slight murmurs around here. I am awake.

"Love, here's your son." My husband lays a warm bundle next to me and brings one of my arms around it. I open my eyes and struggle to uncross them for a moment. I begin to focus on the room I am in. A white haze surrounds everything in the room. I've been here before. My husband stands next to me. He has a smile on his face I've never seen before. I look into the bundle my husband has placed beside me. I look into the eyes that are staring back at me. My first child to gaze into my eyes. I remember now. I remember why I'm here. I remember why I was put onto this earth. The purpose of my existence has been made undeniably clear. Any heartbreak I have ever felt, any moment of self-doubt, any moment of fear, every single minute of pain was worth this very moment. There is a beauty beyond everything inside of my arms and it is looking right back into my soul. I feel no pain but a warm ache in my heart. I move my hand and am able to hold him and pull him closer to me.

I smile, I breathe. I say hello to my son.

Wallpaper

Sarah immediately pitied him. Not in a place like this, she thought, give yourself some dignity. At least in a place with respect where you won't feel so low when you remember this. Jason looked so hopeful sitting across from her, holding that little blue box as if it was the only thing keeping him alive. She looked at the ring. Not bad, she thought, he did a good job.

He obviously put some thought into this. This shitty Chinese restaurant was where they had gone for their first date. That was three years ago. And yet, he remembered. Sarah laughed inside at this stunning accomplishment by a male. And Jesus, that

God-awful wallpaper witnessing this event. It had been there three years ago and it was still there now. Grayish brown with one of those vertical patterns of faded red and darker gray Chinese fans that varied in size and were only accompanied by some little squiggly u-shaped lines behind them. Jason had commented on the wallpaper on that first date. He joked that he expected their date to go badly but the wallpaper looked like it would absorb all the bad energy and give them a break. Here they were, three years later. But now there were no breaks this time. Hardly any breathing.

Sarah had always told him that she would never marry. She had seen too many marriages fail. Her parents, her grandparents, her friends. Hell, today's society was one in which over fifty percent of all marriages failed. Sarah refused to promise her life and love to someone when it had less than half a chance of surviving. No way, she had always thought, not for me.

And Jason, sweet Jason. He was the best thing that had ever happened to her. He was the funniest guy she had ever known and yet he made love like a French poet. She was able to sleep with him, which was a big deal to her. Insomnia had always troubled her and it was worse whenever the occasional boyfriend accompanied her or when her best friend would sleep over. But it was different with Jason. It was as if her mind went completely lucid and there was nothing to be afraid of. Nothing mattered except the nuzzling of her head on his chest right underneath his chin and feeling his breath on her forehead, the warmth of his body like a lullaby.

Jason always humored Sarah's objection to marriage. He always said that it was okay if that was how she felt, but he didn't believe it. This always annoyed her but at least he wouldn't argue with her. Sarah was stubborn when it came to her opinions about herself and refused to argue them. No one could ever change them. Jason had never been able to change her mind about murder mysteries, or making her own clothes, or how she liked her steak well done. Sarah liked herself, and no one, especially a man, was going to change her, let alone marry her.

Faster than she could believe, Sarah flashed back to that first date with Jason. How after he had kissed her on the cheek and gone home, how after she had told Rebecca on the phone every detail of the date and gone to bed herself, how she had woken up around five a.m. (another insomnia bout) and couldn't stop thinking about him. She was feeling nauseous and figured it was the greasy Chinese. But smiled at the possibility that it could be nerves about this new guy. He called her a half hour later to tell her he had woken from a dream that he was Adam and she was the apple. Sarah had pretended he had woken her up. Most guys seemed bothered by her insomnia. Like it would be a challenge to get her to bed or something.

And now Sarah was about to change their lives forever. She would officially have been proposed to and Jason would officially be rejected. She supposed they would break up after this night. That bothered her. Sarah loved Jason more than she had expected to ever love anyone. It was weird because everyday, she loved him more. She hated when they didn't get to see each other for a day or two. The longest they had ever been separated was for six days. Sarah kept saying it was always good to have space even in the strongest relationships but secretly missed him so much she had actually listened to slow love songs on the fourth night. She never would have thought on that night or any other that this day would come.

Sarah looked up from the ring into Jason's eyes. God, not here with this hideous wallpaper. He will forever remember this wallpaper and never eat at this restaurant again. This will be dark and forbidden, a cave that seems to breathe and moan with bones scattered around the entrance. Jason lost his hopeful smile suddenly. She wondered how much time had passed. Had she made it completely obvious she was trying to find a nice way to say no? Or did she seem too emotional to say yes? He looked confused. Then a second later, worried. Then another second, hurt. Sarah panicked. She couldn't bear to hurt him. She hated when he was upset. Even when they were fighting and he was in the wrong. She couldn't stand it when he was angry or sad. She had never seen him cry and was afraid he was about to. She looked at the ring again. I could say yes and play along for a while, she thought. At least the moment won't be ruined. I could break the engagement in a month or so. Just don't break his heart, not here, not now, not with this horrid wallpaper to commemorate the event.

A match lit inside Sarah's head. This wallpaper may not have been designed for this restaurant. It was probably designed by some fat gay white man in the early eighties to give his living room an oriental touch and they just made too much of it. So how did it end up here? This was a small restaurant but it was on every wall from top to bottom. It looked like it spread to the kitchen as well. It was everywhere. And suddenly, it was pretty to Sarah. It was the prettiest wallpaper she had ever seen. How could any moment ever by ruined with such pretty wallpaper around? It motivated her. This wallpaper, this hideous gray wallpaper with its redundant pattern of upside down and sideways fans was the most beautiful wallpaper she had ever seen. It may not have been made for this place, but here it was. The manufacturer never thought it would end up in this place, but it did. It was meant for this place. Jason was meant for her. She was meant for Jason. Here in this shitty Chinese restaurant, with this shitty beautiful wallpaper. Here and now. Nothing else mattered. She didn't care if she never slept again as long as she could always try with her head nuzzled on his chest below his chin with his breath on her forehead.

That night, their lives were changed forever. That was the night the girl who never thought she would marry somehow found herself truly wanting it more than anything she had ever known. That night, she said yes.

Sessions

How am I coping?

Uh, I'm coping…I'm coping okay. I mean, I'm
doing as well as can be expected. Is it as *well* as? Or
as *good* as? I don't know. I'm okay.

No, no nightmares, no. I do have this
recurring dream though. It started right after she
died. I'm walking along the beach at dawn. And the
sky is all rose colored. And all you can hear is the
water and some seagulls. My jeans are rolled up at
the bottom and I'm walking along the water's edge.

And suddenly, there's my mother standing
about three feet from the water. She looks as if she's
having a private psychic discussion with the ocean,
you know, like they share some wonderful secret and
they're discussing it quietly so no one else can hear.

She's in her underwear – I told you about that didn't I? My beach vacation like five years ago when she did this? Yeah, I told you.

Anyway, she's in her underwear and bra, wearing her glasses of all things and just looks as happy as she can be, big ole smile on her face. She looks over at me and waves like I'm her next-door neighbor or something. You know, big enough to be noticed but small enough to only say 'so good to see you out walking again, it's good for your heart.' And I wave back but she doesn't see because she's already turned away. She's got her hands on her hips and she's just taking it all in. The pink sky, the salty air, the mist blowing off the water. I see her inhale the air deeply, like it's the best, freshest air she's ever tasted. Then she suddenly just starts running into the water. Just goes for it. I freak out and run after her, calling after her. She just dives into that water and starts breast stroking it like it's the good ole days and she's swimming in the old lake by the farm or something.

I run to where she was originally standing and keep calling after her. I walk into the water, step by step. And, of course, in the dream I can't swim (since dreams have to fuck with you so much) so I can't go in after her. I can't go any deeper than a foot or two. And my jeans are just getting soaked from the splash of the waves, and they're getting heavier and heavier. And I keep thinking they're going to fall off so I gradually start stepping backwards towards the sand. Mom just keeps swimming. I keep shouting after her, but she just keeps going. The whole time the sun is rising and by now, the sky is white and there's golden light all over the beach.

47

I'm still thinking my jeans are going to fall off, so I'm holding onto the belt loops as tightly as I can. She's so far out, like two hundred feet but I can see her as if she were only twenty feet away. Again, the dream fucking with me. I'm getting to the point where I'm going to cry because I don't know what else to do. And she stops and turns her body. She kind of floats on her back like an otter for a second because she knows they're my favorite. And then she just waves to me. She waves goodbye. But I shout out to her, 'Mom, where are you going?' And I hear her shout back 'To the store.' Whatever that means, fucking dreams. And then she turns her body back out to sea and swims away. And suddenly, I'm okay with her going that far because I know the store is out there and I start walking towards the dry sand. I keep looking over my shoulder as if she were my sixteen year old taking the car out for the first time.

Then I'm suddenly on the back porch of our beach house watching her through binoculars. I watch her swim past the buoy, the seals taking no notice of her. It's suddenly sunset and the sky is getting rosy again. I'm getting worried that it'll be dark soon and I won't be able to see her in the dark. I'm worried that she won't find her way to whatever store she's going to and she's going to drown in the dark ocean, left only for sea creatures to live off of. And then, I wake up.

Well, at first I'm worried. I'm still in the dream state and I'm thinking that I can't see her because of the darkness. Then I'm angry because I remember that night at the beach when that whole situation happened. And then I wind up laying in bed for a while unable to get back to sleep because I'm regretting that I ever left that night and how I would have stayed if I would have known it would've been my last time with her there. I mean, she didn't actually swim out to sea. But that whole night was just awful for me. I felt like every parent must feel when their child hasn't come home and it's forty-five minutes past curfew. I left that night with a mixture of feelings, a *potpourri* if you will. Man, that's a dumb ass expression.

Oh sure, I talked to her about it. I mean, I didn't talk to her at first, for a month or so. I had to get the rage out of my system first. I didn't want to explode on her, you know. When I was ready, we talked. And as time passed, we talked about it more. I guess I never got over it. I'd never been that angry at her before. Never. Until now. Not like it's her fault she died. I just wish she could have had more will power to stay alive, to win.

I think that maybe that was her approach to heaven. Like if there really is a heaven, that's how she went. She didn't believe in heaven. But maybe that was her own personal vision. Maybe that's how it happened for her. I hope so, anyway. I don't know. To get to swim out to the ocean at dawn, down to your skivvies at your most vulnerable, with your glasses so you can see clearly (of course, in heaven you don't even need glasses to see clearly), anxious and antsy, with just one person there to back you up in case you need a little help, a little push, completely unafraid. Completely aware and comfortable that it's your time. She always seemed ready for death. Always seemed like she felt it was following her, not to scare or taunt her, but just so she could get to know it's face and wouldn't be alarmed when it woke her in the middle of the night.

Oh, God, of *course* I miss her. It's like I'm still expecting the phone to ring, and it'll be her blah blah blahing about whatever. And before I know it, I can't wait to get off the phone because she's driving me up the fucking wall.

So yeah, I can't sleep right now. I wish I could. I'm so tired at work that I can't focus. I can't get anything organized or finished; my laundry, my shopping, it's all gone out the fucking window. It's all gone out to the fucking sea. And when I get to bed my energy finally starts popping because I'm officially still and I'm not trying to focus on any of that shit so that's when my head starts fucking with me. The bullshit never stops moving inside my head.

Mom used to have trouble sleeping. She always woke easily, she could fall asleep fast but she would wake up at the slightest meow of the cat, or position shift from my dad, shit like that. Her legs would twitch or the air conditioning would turn off. But she always got up in the morning, bright and early and raring to go.

I think I need a vacation. I need some time away where I can really get into my grief. Where I can cry and scream and curse and run naked through the wild and verbally abuse the moon and sun and stars. Blame them for stealing her away from me. And then go back to the beach, to the exact place where we went, to where she ran into the ocean, to where the frustration began, to the time when I was so upset, I left my mother in the middle of the night because I couldn't bear to look at her. And then I will run into the ocean. I will wait until midnight and run and feel the freezing water on my burning skin, watch the moonlight shine on the water like silver at it's finest. I will lose my inhibitions, wait for the undertow to take me so I'll have an excuse to go out further. And I will think of that night and wonder if this is what she was feeling when she was out there. Like a fish or a nymph or some goddess of the night. Like nothing else matters but feeling the slush of the sand underneath my feet and the swirling water around my hips. Being back in the womb of the world that gave me life. Let it steal my breath, dull my sight, soften my hearing. Make me just another part of its vastness so that I'm just a speck in this part of the world in this part of the universe. Make it so that I am nothing other than a cell in the body of Earth.

I wonder where she is now. I wish I could sleep. That's the only time I get to see my mommy. I love seeing her. I wish I could sleep forever. Maybe then she and I could walk along the water's edge and eat ice cream cones and talk about boys and clothes until the sun comes up and goes back down again.

Or at least until I wake up.

Gossip

Gladys - Oh, Agnes, have you heard about Nora?

Agnes – I have not. What happened?

G – Well, it seems that she went to the doctor again…

A – Uh huh…

G – And not only was she not pregnant again, but the

doctor informed her that she is unable to even *have* children.

A – Oh, Gladys, that's just awful.

G – Imagine, trying and trying for almost six years and just now they're finding this out.

A – Tragic.

G – So anyway, she goes home, devastated of course. She makes a big spaghetti dinner.

A – Oh, Dan's favorite.

G – Uh huh. She gets out that expensive bottle of wine the Dorman's got them for their wedding.

A – Oh, that wonderful Cabernet.

G – Yes, that's the one. And she gets out candles and the nice china.

A – Boy, she's really trying to soften the blow, isn't she?

G – Definitely. So he comes home and it's been raining. This was last Friday.

A – Oh, it rained so hard that night.

G – Oh, I know. And he was soaked and she rushed to him and took his coat and briefcase.

A – Oh, isn't that adorable.

G – *So* adorable. Anyway, so she sits him down and fills his belly, gets him nice and relaxed.

A – Uh huh.

G – And then, as soon as dinner is over, just like that, BOOM! She spills the beans.

A – Oh my! What did he do?

G – Well, I'll tell you. He just sits there, practically dumbfounded. Just sits there not saying a word.

A – Oh, poor guy.

G – Can you believe it? So Nora sits there and waits for him to say something. And when he finally does, it's not good.

A – Oh, Lord, I hope it wasn't what I think it was.

G – Oh, it was worse. First he asks her what the problem is.

A – All right…

G – Then, he blames her for being infertile.

A – NO!

G – YES! He actually asks her 'what's wrong with you?'

A – He didn't?

G – He did!

A – That's just awful!

G – And when she tells him what the doctor said and maybe it's a sign that they're not supposed to have children, well he looks her square in the eye and tells her that it must be a sign that they're not supposed to be together because gosh dang it, he's meant to be a father, he's supposed to have children. He's supposed to have sons that he can play baseball with, and fix up old cars with, and pass his very namesake onto.

A – Oh, poor Nora.

G – Oh, the gall of that man, for being so insensitive.

A – It's not her fault she's barren. It's her misfortune.

G – Absolutely. And so after he says that, he gets up from the table, takes the last drink of wine from his glass, and says he'll be filing for divorce first thing Monday morning.

A – Oh, the poor thing. What is she going to do?

G – Oh I just can't possibly imagine. All alone, soon

to be unmarried, barren. No man is ever going to want to marry her again.

A – I agree. Men do not like women with a past.

G – Absolutely not. Oh, the nerve of that man!

A – Making her so undesirable. We should send her something to make her feel better.

G – You know, that's a good idea. Some flowers or some balloons, something to cheer her up.

A – Absolutely.

G – Lord knows she could use some cheering up. Her life is practically over.

A – Oh, I know.

G – Hmmm. It's just such a pity, such a shame. A perfectly nice girl like that without a husband to call her own, without a child to love her. Thank God for my Harold.

A – And for my Fred. I don't know what my life would be like without him and my children.

G – None of us would know. What else is there to life?

A – Hmmm.

G – Really makes you think, doesn't it?

A – It certainly does.

G – It really makes you think.

In Passing

As she hurried back to her car, she glanced at her watch. Only 12:15. That gave her plenty of time to get everything done. When she looked back up, she saw him: *the guy*. The guy that came into her work a few times a week and always waited for her to help him. The guy she had been flirting with enough that all of the girls accused her of being in junior high again. The guy she had secretly been dreaming about. She didn't realize he worked this close to her work. Frantically, here mind raced.

Oh God, it's him! What do I do? Does he see me?
Oh, shit, I <u>cannot</u> say hi. If I say hi, it's going to lead to
flirting. Open flirting.   On-the-street-in-broad-daylight
flirting. It's going to be completely non-obligatory since
we're not at my work and I don't have to be nice to him.
Completely voluntary flirting, which makes it practically
illegal. Shit, Rick is going to kill me if he ever finds out
about this guy. How can I flirt with this guy every single
time he comes into my work and not feel guilty about it? I
don't understand; if I've been living with my sweet
boyfriend for years now, how could I possibly want to flirt
with this guy? Man, he just does something for me. He's
so cute in that rebellious sort of way. His punk rock hair,
his band, those fucking eyes. They almost pierce right
through me every time he looks at me. I wish I were
wearing my boots. It makes me seem more important when
I make a sound as I walk. They make me look taller, too.
Well, he's pretty short though. Man, I've never seen him
out like this. I'm always sitting behind the counter and he
seems so much taller. God, wouldn't it be great to have one
night, just one night where I go and see his band play and I
go backstage after the show. We go get some drinks, maybe
go back to his place. Or we could go to my place. Rick
would have to be gone. Like he ever goes anywhere. No,
we'd go to his place. I've always preferred the atmosphere
of a guy's place. It's so much more sexual than your own.
It's not what you wake up to and walk through every single
day. It's something new and exciting and mysterious. I
wonder how big his bed is. Oh, God he is so cute! He
must've just come from my work. I wonder if he asked
about me. And I look like shit today. I haven't even taken
a shower since yesterday morning or the night before.
Fuck, I don't even remember. The joys of living with
someone you're committed to. Should I have committed to

that? I mean, here comes this gorgeous guy that makes me blush, I mean actually makes me blush when he smiles at me and every night I go home to the same boring person. Well, the person isn't that boring, but the sex is. God, is the sex boring. Okay, okay, have I committed myself to someone who is always interesting enough but lousy in the sack? Orgasm, schmorgasm. I want someone that puts my hands over my head and his tongue in my ear. Head, yeah, speaking of head. What is it again? It's been so long, I've completely forgotten. I bet this guy does that stuff. I bet he loves taking a girl back to his mysterious place, soaking her in his wild atmosphere and going down on her before making intense and passionate love to her. What I wouldn't give just to have that again. At least have the option. So, what? Do I break up with Rick? The guy that I have moved in with and have found myself getting less and less turned on by him week after week? I can't afford to live on my own. So do I stay with someone who makes it feel like I'm sharing a bed with my best friend, and that's about it? All for the sake of splitting the rent? Or do I say hi, open a window and start something that can only end with messy results? Keep looking straight ahead. Don't look over. Tunnel vision, tunnel vision, too many things on my mind to notice anything else. Oh God. Is that rude? Is he going to ask me about it next time he comes in? Am I going to feel awkward? Are the girls going to know that I'm lying to him if I tell him I didn't see him? Should I have said hi? Should I have opened the window? Shit, maybe it's time to buy a new house. Or just close the curtains completely.

She glanced at her watch again, 12:16. Plenty of time to get everything done.

Sweet Water

The first girl's body was found early Christmas morning at around 6:45.

An avid jogger had escaped the sleeping lull of his family just before waking to the chaos of rushing to open present after present. He had seen the body from only a few yards away at first and couldn't decide if it was a dead dog or a dirty piece of wood. Once he reached her and discovered the reality, he vomited violently.

Her naked pale body was covered in patches of frost and dried blood. He took off as fast as he could to find the nearest house, leaving the body once again to defend itself against the wintery elements.

It's not somethin' I would have ever expected to happen in this humdrum town. Here in Agua Dulce, everybody knows everybody else. We're all pretty much next-door neighbors in this town, all seven hundred or so of us. So to think that some poor girl could get raped and killed by one of her neighbors, well, it just don't make any sense.

I had to shush my mama from cursin' while we watched the news that mornin'. My niece Winnie was at that age where she was startin' to pick up words and repeat 'em. After the fourth "poor fuckin' family" line that come outta my mama's mouth, I about snapped my neck offa my shoulders turnin' at her so fast, tellin' her to hush up. A few minutes later my brother Randolph finally shuffled his way in through the front door. Leave it to my lowlife of a brother to come in hung-over on Christmas mornin', missin' out on such an important holiday with his baby daughter.

He lived in the old trailer that our folks had lived in when they first got married years back. It had long since rusted and was now parked on the east side of our house. When Winnie's mama died from pneumonia about six months prior or so, Randolph left her in the main house with us and moved all his clothes to that stinky, dusty trailer. Mama didn't seem to mind, but, honestly, it drove me up the wall. It meant that I was the one that was gonna take care of that baby, not him.

My mama refused to help out with baby Winnie and Randolph was more often than not a no-show on any given day. So that left me with a quick two year old, dirtyin' her diapers and pickin' up curse words faster than the speed of light. So on that mornin', he and I had our usual debate over stale coffee. I wanted to know when he was gonna grow up and take responsibility for his daughter and he wanted me to stay outta his business.

After Mama reamed him somethin' awful, Randolph argued his way out of it all with the same old excuse. He'd been down at Hunter's (of course), the bar which he always drank himself stupid at every single night, with his friend Larry Al. They were best friends and had been since middle school and hardly ever did anything without the other. Randolph said that they had to teach a lesson to some snotty shitheads that had come in from Austin and "thought they owned the bar, for fucks sake!" The trickle of blood on his shirt and the reek of booze and cigarettes just showed me that my brother, thirty-one and father to a gorgeous little baby girl, was never gonna grow up and get out of here. He was probably gonna go to that bar every night for the rest of his life and teach lessons to more poor souls. Hell, he was probably gonna die in that damn bar.

Not like anyone really gets outta this town anyways. Matter of fact, my daddy's the only person I ever heard of not comin' back here. You can throw a stone from one end of this town to the other, and it takes about that long to come back once you get to thinkin' you're gone for good.

*   *   *

Our daddy left Mama before we were born. Matter of fact Mama had only just found out she was

63

havin' us twins not more than a week or so before he took off with some other woman for California. He never came back to meet us, never sent her a check, never did nothin'. He just up and left and abandoned everything that they had, us included. She never got over that. To this day, in some way, I know she resents us for the entire thing.

She made ends meet cleanin' probably every single house there is in this town. She couldn't afford daycare so she always brought us along with her. Can you imagine that? Two cryin', screamin', poopin' babies that she couldn't really tend to since she had to hurry and clean as many houses a day as she could. Nowadays she says she absolutely cannot stand the sound of a cryin' baby. It's no big guess as to why.

So every day, I tended to my niece. I pretended my brother was a deadbeat daddy, just like ours. It hurt to think that. I mean, at least he was still livin' on the property and hadn't left the state or anything. Nevertheless, he was never around to change her or put her to bed. Randolph, he was always just a fuck up.

*   *   *

It was that night that I had the first dream. Screamin', clawin', dirt under my fingernails, pressure and pain. It startled me awake, sweatin' and outta breath.

*   *   *

I've never been happy in this town. I guess I get that from my daddy. Mama said he always

64

wanted to get away from here. She tried to make him want to stay by gettin' pregnant and startin' a family, but that only made him want to leave more. So away he went with some lady from Coppell and they were outta here so fast, Mama didn't know which end was up. She was heartbroken I imagine, but she never talked about it. When I was real little, I'd ask Mama if I could go find Daddy when I grew up. One day after I asked her, she swatted my butt so hard I couldn't sit down for an hour. But I couldn't help it; I didn't like old Agua Dulce. I yearned for somethin' else bigger and busier. I don't know, better than this ol' dust bowl.

The people here aren't the most pleasant of folk. It's hot. It's boring as hell. Like I said, everybody knows each other. I even went to high school with the girl that died on Christmas. We were in the same year and everything. She hung out with some real snobby girls, the kind that wore designer jeans and make-up and were more interested in gettin' felt up than doin' good in school. I always watched them from a distance, eatin' my lunch underneath the broken bleachers that were in the back of the recess field, wonderin' about what made 'em tick.

Now I'm not sayin' she asked for it or anything like that. I'm sayin' people never change in this town. I'll bet the night she got…well, you know, that she was wearin' designer jeans and more make-up than anyone else there that night. She was probably more interested in gettin' attention from some random guy than she was in spendin' any time with her friends.

I'm sure people would take a look at me and

say that I could use a little make-up and some nice clothes, too. But like I said, people here, we never change.

*   *   *

On New Year's night, my friend Tammy Lynn gave me a call at about two in the mornin' and asked for a ride. After makin' up my mind not to mention to her how she had not invited me out with her and the other girls, I agreed to come get her. I had to sneak out of the house so as not to wake Baby Winnie and especially Mama. She would not have even *considered* stayin' home alone with that baby if she knew I was leavin', even if it was only for a half hour or so. After drivin' around the damn parkin' lot at Hunter's for ten minutes, I finally spotted Tammy Lynn and the other girls smokin' with some guys, includin' Larry Al. After gettin' 'em into the car, I gave Larry Al a dirty look. He just looked back at me with this big ol' goofy smile on his face. I couldn't help but laugh even if he did get my brother into trouble all the time. The girls and me finally took off and of course, once we got goin' is when they told me that I had to take all four girls to their separate domiciles. Ain't nobody was stayin' with nobody else, so I got to play taxi to four of my friends who never once asked me what I did that night. I even pulled over twice so Kathy Frances could puke out the back window.

I was furious drivin' back home. At that point it was almost four o'clock in the mornin' and I could only hope that Baby Winnie hadn't woken up cryin' from peein' her diaper or somethin'. I was exhausted and just wanted to go back to bed. I was cursin' my Mama for not ever offerin' to help out once in a while, when I spotted my own good-for-nothin' brother stumblin' home about two miles from our house. I pulled over so hard, that it spooked him and he fell over himself into a nice puddle of muddy gravel. Once he got up and into the car, I just let loose and started cursin' and lecturin' him on bein' a better father, a better son and brother, a better person altogether. I just let him have it. For the rest of the ride home, he just sat there lookin' out the window with me hollerin' at him like I was his mama. And in true fashion, he just shrugged me off and bitched about a headache he got from getting hit in the head by some oaky down at Hunter's. That was the first time I actually looked over at him. I noticed the blood around his eye and mouth, his shirt pocket was torn.

With him sittin' there in my car, all bloodied up, wet with mud, stinkin' of stale beer and cigarettes, I just shook my head and pulled up the driveway. "I rest my case," is all I could say to him. Then I turned off the engine and got out, leavin' him by himself in the car.

* * *

I had another dream that night. I remember all the noises were muffled. I felt an allover weight holdin' me down and surroundin' me, like bein' wrapped too tight in a blanket. I startled awake again and this time I ran to the bathroom because I thought I was gonna puke. I only had a couple dry heaves though.

* * *

I told Mama about the dream over lunch the next day. "Did you watch the news?" she asked me when I was done tellin' her. I hadn't and was irritated that she would change the subject so quickly. But then she told me that another girl had been found. This time she still had all her clothes on but they were all ripped up. Her nose and jaw were broken and her underwear was gone. Mama looked at me all stern-like. "You better start bein' real careful. Makes me nervous to think my baby might be seein' into her own future like that."

I poked at my sandwich. Truth be told, it was alarmin' to hear Mama be so concerned. That puke feelin' was comin' back. I stood up and walked to the trashcan and threw my sandwich away. From the livin' room, Baby Winnie was cursin' at her toys, "Damn! Damn! Damnit!"

*   *   *

I stayed up to watch the ten o'clock news. I didn't want Mama thinkin' she had scared me, so I stayed up in my room instead of goin' to sleep after puttin' Baby Winnie down. When I heard Mama's door close, I went out to the livin' room real quiet and turned on the TV.

It was the first story of the night. The reporter was talkin' about the connection between the two girls that had been killed. He was right there where the second girl was found, Jenna Lu Samson. She was the daughter of the owner of the grocery store three blocks up. She was only nineteen. I felt so bad for her; she was so young.

The reporter was talkin' about where the girl

had been the night before. She was out celebratin' the New Year with some girlfriends. They were barhoppin' and dancin' and just out enjoyin' the whole night. One of the friends had said that they were all pretty drunk when they realized that Jenna Lu had disappeared. But bein' as drunk as they were, they all just decided that she must've gone home with some guy or hopped a ride with someone else. They didn't give it two thoughts that somethin' terrible might have happened to her.

I started thinkin' about what goes through a young girl's head as she's gettin' raped. She probably thought he liked her after he had told her she was pretty. Maybe she believed him, maybe she was just lonely. Did she have any idea in the back of her head he might do this to her? Was she too drunk to know better? Maybe she hated herself and thought she deserved it. Things like that. Kinda morbid, I guess.

The camera switched back and forth from the reporter in the station to the live reporter. The live reporter was answerin' some question from the other one when somethin' stood out behind him. A spark went off inside my head. It was like that feelin' you get when you fall off a step real quick and almost completely fall over but you don't, like that. I noticed Randolph's truck parked several feet away from the reporter, just at the top of the screen.

There were other cars parked around. It wasn't a deserted area by any means so it could have been anyone's truck. But Randolph was of course down at the bar that night, which was nowhere near where the reporter was. It wouldn't have made any sense that he walked from there.

My mind raced back to the night before when I found Randolph stumblin' home. I hadn't even thought as to why he was walkin'. He'd walked home drunk plenty a' times before. Then I remembered his truck wasn't out front that morning. I looked at the truck on the screen real hard but I couldn't make out the license plate or see any identifyin' marks. It could have been anybody's truck. But for some reason, my stomach dropped out from under me and I felt like I had to make sure.

I grabbed my keys, put on my shoes and slipped out the door as quietly as I could. By the time I reached my car, I was startin' to get nervous. One of the hardest things I've ever done was drive away from my house that night as calmly as I could so as not to wake anybody inside.

The spot was only about ten minutes from my house but I couldn't get there fast enough. My mind kept goin' over the night before. The blood on Randolph's face, his torn shirt pocket, dirt and mud all over him, the sick stench of beer soaked cigarette butts. I tried goin' over our conversation in my mind but I couldn't remember anything. I was so mad that night that I don't think even I paid much attention to what *I* said. Couldn't remember if he had said anything about his truck. Had I?

All the TV vans were gone when I got to the spot. There was yellow tape attached to some posts, blockin' off a small space about twenty feet or so from the road. It was quiet out there. There were still several cars parked around but nobody was in sight. No noise, no people, just dirt and the moon.

Then I saw it: Randolph's truck, parked at the

top of a direct path to the spot where Jenna Lu Samson's body was found. I could make out the dent in the back bumper and broken tail light from when my damned drunk brother decided to back his truck out from the house without lookin' behind him and ran right into my car. Put a fuckin' shark bite shaped dent in my tire well. There were some paint cans in the bed from a job he got fired from a few months back. Two gunshot sized holes in the windshield from tearing through some rocky back-roads with Baby Winnie's mama two years ago.

It could have been anybody's truck. But it wasn't. It was Randolph's. I swallowed the lump in my throat and headed back home, hopin' Mama was still sleepin', and wonderin' where the hell Randolph was at that moment.

*   *   *

I did not sleep well that night. Kept wakin' up at the slightest noise, thinkin' Randolph was comin' into the main house. I must've checked on the baby four times that night. The next mornin' was a blur. It went by with coffee and breakfast, my mother cussin' and my niece copyin', this time it was the F word (thank you Mama). I couldn't figure out if I should say somethin' to Randolph or not. I just kept goin' over and over in my head New Year's night.

I put Baby Winnie down for her nap around noon. When I came out, Mama was sittin' on the couch watchin' Maury Povich of all things (she loves that damn show) and I sat down next to her. "Mama, I gotta... I gotta ask you somethin'," I said. Not lookin' at me, she spit out "What?!" like I had been sayin' her name over and over or somethin'. "Do you think-" I paused for a second, not sure how to word it. "Do you think Randolph is dangerous?" She scoffed and looked at me with a terrible look of doubt. I began to feel a little silly for askin' such a thing. Then she grabbed the remote and muted a woman tellin' Maury that she was 110% positive that *this* guy was the father of her two year old son. "Did I ever tell you about the time your brother was arrested?" She had not.

"When you kids were fifteen, you were invited to Suzy Bee's birthday party. 'Member that? Well, you got the flu so you couldn't go. But your fuckin' brother snuck out while I was sleepin' and went over to her house and tapped on that girl's window. Scared the bejeezus out of those poor girls! Well, I guess he had a crush on Suzy Bee or somethin' like that. All the girls were flirtin' with him *except* her and he made all of them kiss him. Well, Suzy Bee wouldn't do it. So he asked her to come outside and sit with him so they could talk. She went out there after the other girls had gone to sleep and they sat in her front yard and while they were talkin', he pounced on her. He just went after her like she was his prey. He started grabbin' her and kissin' her everywhere. Well, Suzy Bee's little sister was spyin' on them and saw what he was doin' and woke their daddy up who went out there with his shotgun while her mama called the police. They showed up and arrested him and even kept him overnight. Well, I went over there next day and apologized and swore up and down he'd never bother their daughter again if they just wouldn't tell nobody 'bout it. I even offered to clean their house every week for free. They only said he better not ever come around again or her daddy would shoot a hole clean through his head. I promised he wouldn't, and he never did."

I was beside myself with shock. I asked her why she hadn't ever told me about this. "Well, I didn't want you tellin' any of your fuckin' friends, and they tell their friends, and more parents start findin' out. I wouldn't ever get another job in this town if that happened. What would we have done then? Hell, your father wasn't helpin' out, that's for fuckin' sure."

I just sat there, I couldn't say anything. I just sat there and stared at the floor with my mouth hangin' wide open. It never dawned on me that my brother could ever be that kind of person. Not in a million years would I have ever imagined somethin' like that.

Mama picked the remote back up and turned the volume back on. As the guests started cheerin' for paternity results, she gave an impatient sigh, "Some secrets stay in the family."

*   *   *

That was the longest day I have ever known. Randolph had some mechanic work at some truck yard so he was gone all day. I kept fiddlin' around the house tryin' to keep my mind busy, doin' this and that, tryin' to prepare myself for..... well, whatever might come out of his mouth if I confronted him.

Hours passed. Evening came. I cleaned. I cooked. I couldn't sit and watch TV. I felt like if I sat still for too long the words would force themselves outta my mouth like the devil escapin' after an exorcism. The thought of drivin' down to Hunter's to see if Randolph was there was passin' through my head when he finally walked in the front door. "I'm fuckin' starvin'!" he announced.

I stirred Mama awake so she would go to bed. She grunted and shot Randolph a dirty look, then shot one over at me. "S'about time you got your goddamn ass home. That baby a' yours been cryin' all fuckin' night," Mama heavily slurred. She must have been dreamin' because Winnie had been real good that night. I don't even think Randolph heard her though. She just heaved herself off the couch and scuffled into her room without even sayin' goodnight.

Once I heard her door close, I took a deep breath and braced myself. I got off the couch and walked to the kitchen, stoppin' myself suddenly at the table. How the hell was I gonna to do this? What was I gonna say? He glanced at me while makin' a sandwich. "What's your problem?" he asked. I couldn't organize my head. My thoughts were swimmin' like fish upstream. I wasn't sure if I should be coy or outright. Maybe I should ask him about his truck first. Maybe I should start cryin'.

"BECKY JEAN!" he shouted at me. I came back to where I was standin' and my mind went blank. I looked into his eyes.

"Nothin.' Goodnight," I said. I turned and walked away into my room. He scoffed under his breath and I knew he was shaking his head at me. I couldn't fall asleep until I knew he was done eatin' and out of the main house, back into that rusty ramshackle trailer.

74

*   *   *

My dream that night was as strange as the others.
Sounds were distant and echoin', and I was
underwater. My lungs and throat were tight. I tried
to swim up and out. Bubbles floated from my mouth
to the surface, where they broke into the air and then
everything went silent and dark.

*   *   *

I went back to work the next day. I tried to
smile at all the patients but I just couldn't. I kept
givin' the doctor the wrong charts. One of the girls
had to come fetch me from lunch; I'd gone over
twenty minutes. My dreams were hauntin' me. Why
was I dreamin' these things? I couldn't figure out if it
had somethin' to do with me bein' scared that I was
next or somethin'. None of this seemed real at all. I
was startin' to get scared to go to sleep at night.
Mama was cookin' dinner when I got home.
She bitched for a few minutes about her back and the
baby. My brother wasn't there, she said he was
workin' a paintin' job on the east side of town. Baby
Winnie made a mess of her mashed potatoes while I
ate in silence. Mama just watched the TV while she
ate. That's all she ever does anyways. I put the baby
to bed around eight o'clock. Mama fell asleep on the
couch 'bout an hour after that. I woke her to send her
to bed then sent myself shortly after. To my surprise I
fell right to sleep. Guess all that thinkin' wore me
out. I dreamt that Winnie was wearing a swimsuit
made out of mashed potatoes.

*   *   *

I woke up feelin' sick to my stomach around three in the mornin'. I took my time walkin' to the bathroom to trick my body into feelin' fine, but I puked a few minutes later anyway. After rinsin' my mouth out in the sink, I went to the kitchen for a glass of water. I filled the glass at the kitchen tap and looked out the window above it. The night was cold and quiet, peaceful.

Just above the window's ledge was the view of Randolph's trailer. A dim light was on inside and the door had been left ajar. He wasn't anywhere around outside though and I didn't see any movement inside the trailer. Can't say it seemed odd for him to be up at this hour. The water overflowed from the glass onto my hand and I realized how long I had been starin'. I turned off the tap, wiped my hand dry and walked to the front door.

Our house was built on top of an old garage so there were broken-down cars every which way you looked in our yard. I took the stairs down slowly so as to quiet their old creak and looked around at rusted metal skeletons. When we were kids, Randolph and I used to play hide and seek in 'em. Matter of fact, my first kiss was in an old 1951 Ford F-150 'round back. Maybe Randolph was hidin' in one of them cars now.

My bare feet felt the cold ground underneath. A quick winter breeze blew up my nightgown, and I felt goose bumps rise all over my body. As I got closer to the trailer door, I paused, tryin' to find a way out of havin' this awful conversation. I glanced up and saw a crescent moon in the sky, looked around at the bare trees and empty cars. No, I had to do this.

So I grabbed the handle to the door, pulled it halfway open and glanced inside.

Randolph's feet were what I saw first. He was sittin' right there at the dinette, facin' the front door. But I just kept lookin' down at his feet. I didn't want to meet his eyes but I knew I had to. I started lookin' up and saw his arms, his chest, then his face. There was blood all over him. His hands, his sleeves, specks on his cheeks and lips. He'd been cryin' too. Tear stains cut into a coat of dust on his face like they were painted on. We locked eyes and froze in our spots. That's when I knew: those dreams I'd been havin', they *were* about those girls. I wasn't predictin' their deaths. I wasn't predictin' my own. I wasn't predictin' anything. I had been seein' what Randolph was seein'. I was feelin' what he was feelin'. My twin brother and I, we were connected. Our dreams with our lives, intertwined. And I knew.

He looked down at his hands again and started cryin'. I stammered out what I could of "What have you done?" once or twice. He just kept cryin'. He held his hands up over his head like he was showin' God what he had done. "Where is she?" I asked him in a whisper. He just shook his head. A tear dropped off his chin. He wiped his face with his sleeve. It got rid of the tear tracks but left a blood smear. He stopped cryin' and he sniffled real hard and swallowed.

"Go back inside, Becky Jean. Go back to sleep." "I- I can't just walk away...." I was too stunned to say anything else. "Go. Don't tell Mama", he said. "Don't ever let Winnie know."

I couldn't tell you how I did it, but I backed out

down those stairs and started to shut the door. Randolph's head dropped to his chest and he took another hard sniffle. I let the handle go and lock in its place, and heard him start to sob again. I turned and walked real calm back to the main house, up the stairs and through the front door. I locked it behind me, and went back to bed. Somehow sleep came quickly, but there were no more dreams.

*   *   *

I woke up the next mornin' to Baby Winnie cryin' and Mama shoutin' from the livin' room. Some men were at the door lookin' for Randolph, but he was already gone.

*   *   *

I was makin' dinner the other day when Mama called me into the livin' room. She sounded so damned panicked that I rushed in there thinkin' Winnie had knocked herself out or somethin'. Instead she pointed at the TV. A special news report was on.

"….an update in the capture of Randolph Wilkins. He was found just outside of Las Vegas, Nevada last evening where he was identified by a local Agua Dulce resident on vacation. Wilkins was apprehended immediately and has confessed to the killing of just one of the victims so far from the infamous strand of rapes and murders that took place over the Christmas holiday in Agua Dulce, Texas three years ago. You might recall the incident known as the Sweet Water Slashings."

My heart stopped. Good God in Heaven, they found him.

78

I kneeled to the floor to keep from passin' out and stared at the screen. There he was bein' guided out of the police station by two men dressed in suits and ties. Randolph looked thicker than he had last time I saw him. He had put on at least thirty or forty pounds and he had a bushy beard, but it was definitely him. They were escortin' him on either side. His hands were cuffed behind his back and he had on one of those bright orange jumpsuits. He kept lookin' at the camera like it was somebody he knew, and he had this real sad, sorry look on his face. Winnie's voice suddenly broke through my trance. "Mommy," she said, "who is that?"

My brain started processin' the answer I had prepared for this moment. Time slowed as I turned my head to tell her: "Just a man that Mommy knew years and years ago." "Oh," she said, and went back to her colorin' book. I looked back at the TV. They were showin' the police puttin' him into their cruiser. The reporter continued.

"A total of five bodies were found with DNA evidence leading to Wilkins, but he fled his home before authorities could reach him for questioning. It is known that he made his way to California where he worked as a gas station attendant in Bakersfield, then moved on to Las Vegas where he worked as a janitor in a well-known casino. It is with this much anticipated capture that the family members of the victims in Agua Dulce will hopefully find their closure and begin their healing."

I was frozen. I couldn't move or speak. I couldn't do anything but leave my eyes on the screen as the news continued into some story about water pollution somewhere. Randolph was caught. He had confessed. It was over.

"Like I said," Mama mumbled. I turned my head to look at her. "Some secrets stay in the family."

Impending

In the town that I grew up in, there is a
homeless woman that wanders the downtown streets.
She has a shopping cart overloaded with overstuffed
black trash bags. She is short and stocky and wears a
dark colored dress, coat and beanie. She is known as
the Bag Lady. When you mention her name,
everyone knows whom you're referring to and in turn
you know who's being referred to when hearing her
name. She has been around as long as I can
remember. My father told me of a rumor that she was
in his high school graduating class but no one knows
exactly who she was. She keeps her back to the street

so no one can see what she looks like, and no one does.

In the town that I grew up in, there is an anorexic woman that wanders the uptown streets. She has a paper grocery bag overloaded with celery stalks and loaves of bread. She is tall and lanky and wears short shorts and tank tops and headphones. She is known as the Skinny Lady. When you mention her name, everyone knows whom you're referring to and in turn you know who's being referred to when hearing her name. She has been around as long as I can remember. My mother has told me she carries the bags to make people believe she eats but everyone knows the truth. She keeps her face to the street so everyone can see how thin she is, and everyone does.

It is a wonder to me that these women exist. At one point or another in their lives they lost themselves, or perhaps found themselves. Can one woman be so unknown and cold and hungry that if you offered her a meal, she would begin rambling about her endless misfortune? Or if offered a yearbook from 1967, would she turn to a page and show you a picture of a pretty girl with pinned brunette curls and perfect skin and then point to herself and give you a warm, toothless smile? Can one woman be so infamous and cold and angry that if you offered her a meal, she would begin walking faster and look back at you with disgust? Or if offered a ride home, would she kindly accept and tell you the story of where and when she decided she was so physically unattractive that something had to be done about it?

I ponder self-discovery when I think of these

women. I ponder the fact that it takes years upon years to learn who we really are. I see my grandmother and her acceptance of her husband's death from years ago and how she has remained without him since and will have to remain without him until it is her time to go. I see my mother and her acceptance of her parents' deaths over the past thirty years and how she has had to remain without her mother for so long and now, without her father, remain an orphan until it is her time. I see myself and my acceptance that I will never let a man control who I am or what I am supposed to be and may remain unmarried, unmothered and possibly embittered because of that. And I see these two ladies and their acceptance of whatever fate they fell into and how they may remain as such until they die from malnourishment or loneliness.

I know who I am; I know what I want for myself. But I have to find the way to get to where I am supposed to go. My family will pass, I will be alone, but I will have myself and hopefully everything I have ever wanted. I don't yet know what fate holds for me, but damn it, I will find my way. I will have my life and one day, I will hold it in my hands and look at it fondly, turning it over and over again, remembering the shiny parts, all the dents and dings, and fondly recalling just how wonderful it was to make it.

Love Spell

Rhonda locked the bedroom door behind her once they were all inside. All three women carried a purse and a plastic Wal-Mart bag. Becca headed straight for the bed and sat on the left corner, Rhonda's side. Rhonda sat down on the other corner, her husband Ben's side. Donna made her way to the center and sat herself down on the floor between the two pairs of feet.

"You sure Ben isn't going to be home anytime soon?" asked Becca. "Trust me," Rhonda said, "He's out with Brian. He'll be home around two in the morning, smelling of beer and pool cues." "What are you worried about, Becca?" Donna inquired. "Ben's not your husband, he's not going to care what you're doing in here." "I know that Donna, I don't have a husband, remember? That's why we're doing this whole friggin' thing to begin with. Remember?" Becca shot back. Rhonda intervened because Ben would definitely care about what *she* was doing if he walked in on this, so she needed to get started. "You guys, knock it off. Let's do this before we chicken out. Did we all get everything we need?" The girls began sorting through their Wal-Mart bags. "I think so," said Donna. "Absolutely!" exclaimed Becca, "I'm not doing this half-assed!"

Rhonda reached into her purse and pulled out a small purple book. The other two girls retrieved the same book from their own purses. "Love's Magic: Spells to Turn Your Toad into a Real Prince," Becca read. "This is going to be awesome! I hope it works." "How can you expect a book with a picture of a frog being crushed to death by a spiked heel to be worth anything?" said Donna. "This is going to be a fluke." This worried Rhonda. "It can't be a fluke. This book cost me $21.95 plus tax and if Ben finds out that I took it from the swear jar, he's going to kill me." "Possibly," said Donna. "But he's more than likely going to reimburse those funds when he goes off on you." "She has a point," Becca agreed.

Rhonda shrugged off their joke, she wanted to get going. "Whatever, let's just get started." The girls opened their books to the first page and Becca read the directions aloud. "To give the spells their true and full power, you must awake the magic that lies within the pages of this book and yourself. Place your thumb upon the silver star and say 'awaken'." The three girls did as instructed. Donna looked up at her two best friends, the cynicism already shining in her eyes. "That's it?" she asked. "We've activated the magic by placing our goddamn thumbs on this fucking silver star? I could stick my thumb up my ass and activate the magic of anal sex. This is bullshit."

"No it's not!" Becca shouted. "You have to believe in it!" "Oh, I do believe," Donna said. "I believe it's bollocks." Again, Rhonda's impatience grew. "Donna, shut up! Who's going to go first?" Becca raised her eager hand high in the air with a bright smile on her face, like a schoolgirl. "Me! Me! Me! If Robert doesn't marry me soon, I'm going to burst. The sooner the better." "Just burst in that direction," requested Donna, pointing in the opposite direction, "I don't want any pink mist on me."

Becca took her items out of her Wal-Mart bag one by one, listing them out loud. "One white candle. One tube of pink lipstick. One spool of white string. Aaaannnndddddd some dirt." She did a once-over of her items and went back to her spell book for directions. "The Diamond Ring Spell!" "Where do you put the dirt?" Rhonda asked. Becca looked over the directions. "Uh, on the floor....in front of you." "No, no, no. Can't we do this in the kitchen? I just vacuumed!" said Rhonda. Becca jumped up from the bed. "No Rhonda! It's safer in here. If Ben comes home early, we'll be able to hear him so he won't walk right into our coven."

Donna rolled her eyes and looked up at her. "Did you just say coven? Oh man, this is so fucking lame." She tossed the book down on the floor and folded her arms. "Okay fine," Rhonda submitted, "just try to keep the dirt in one small pile." Becca promised and sat on the ground next to Donna. She organized her things, looked over her spell once more, and then recited the directions.

"First, light your candle," she said, reaching for a lighter. She panicked, realizing she hadn't bought one. "Oh shit! I didn't get a lighter. Shit! I knew I was going to forget something! Damn it!" Donna reached into her jeans pocket and retrieved her Zippo. She held it out in front of Becca's face and lit it. Becca, embarrassed by her panic attack, laughed a little and took the lighter. "Oh, look at that. I forgot you smoked. Thanks, Don," she said. "You're welcome." Donna paused before silently adding, "Freak." Becca went back to her spell. She lit the candle, handed the lighter back to Donna and started reading the directions again. "Okay, take three deep breaths to clear your mind." She took three deep, over-exaggerated breaths. The other girls exchanged glances, and looked back at her. "Damn, you want some weed with that inhale?" joked Donna. Rhonda leaned over and smacked her on the shoulder. Becca ignored them and continued.

"Pour a cup of dirt on the ground in front of you and sketch a stick figure of your lover in it." She did as instructed. Rhonda took a sharp breath in as the dirt hit the clean carpet. Now it was Donna's turn to reach over and smack her on the knee. They observed Becca's artistry. "Robert ain't that tall," said Donna. "Yeah, and his head looks REALLY big," Rhonda added. "And did you draw three legs on purpose?" asked Donna, pointing at the mutated stick figure. "You guys, let me focus!" Becca said, ignoring their giggles and pressing on.

"Now, using the pink lipstick, draw a circle on each cheek." She grabbed the lipstick and twisted it up. She drew a round circle on each cheek, filling each one in completely with the waxy goo. This was more than the girls could take and they busted up laughing. "You guys, WHAT?!?" Becca said, confused and irritated that she'd been interrupted yet again. "Sorry," Rhonda barely got it out between snorts. "Yeah, we're so sorry....Raggedy Ann!" said Donna, and she and Rhonda lost it again. "You guys, shut up. This is what I'm supposed to do. So laugh later and let me do this," she told them. The girls quieted down, stifling one or two last snorts. Becca read on. "Now unravel the spool of thread while repeating this chant:

> With virgin white threads,
> And pink rosy cheeks,
> The bond of matrimony
> Is what my heart seeks."

She closed her eyes and repeated the chant a second time. Rhonda and Donna watched intently, waiting for something amazing to happen.

*   *   *

Robert sat on the couch in his standard fashion: remote control in one hand, bottle of beer in the other, watching football. Becca entered from the bedroom carrying a pair of slacks she was sewing and sat down next to him. "I'm almost done hemming your pants, babe," she told him. "Thanks honey. I really appreciate it," Robert said, not even looking in her direction. Becca paused and thought about something for a moment. She put the pants down on the coffee table and turned to him. "Hey Robert, I've been thinking about something," she said. "Oh yeah, what is it?" he said, still not looking at her. She took a deep breath. "Well, we've been living together for a while now, and I was thinking maybe.....we could start talking about....taking the next step," she stammered. Robert did a fist pump for the touchdown on the screen. "What's that, babe?" he asked, before taking a drink.

She took another breath. "Marriage," she calmly said. Robert almost choked on his swig of beer and stopped watching his game. He looked to his girlfriend and wiped his mouth with the back of his hand. "Becca, I don't think we're ready for that yet." "Why not? Robert, we've been together for three and a half years and living together for over a year now. It seems pretty natural that marriage would be the next progression." "Yeah, for other couples," Robert argued. "Not us. We're different, Becca. We're special. That's what makes this relationship so great. We don't need a piece of paper telling us that we love each other."

Becca sighed, she was tired of this broken record of an argument. "Yes, but it's because this relationship is so special that makes me believe we are ready to go to the next level. I mean, neither of us has ever been in a relationship this long," she said, leaning towards him and playing with his hair. "We obviously mean the world to each other. Why not

89

share that with the world?" Robert took another swig of beer before disagreeing. "Honey, just because you stand in front of your friends and family and say you love each other doesn't mean we love each other any more or less than we do right now. I love you, you love me. We know how we feel about each other. What do we have to prove to anybody else?"

"Because, it's – it's what I want," Becca whined. "I want to get married, I want to have our children and grow old with you. I want to wake up to you every single morning." "We do wake up to each other every morning," Robert interrupted, "That's *why* we moved in together. It's wonderful!" He leaned forward, back into his game, leaving Becca staring at the wall. She dropped her hand from his hair and into her lap. She stared at her hand for a moment before looking back up at him. "Robert, I love you so much. But I'm beginning to wonder if you actually love-"

"Becca please, not now. The game is on," the sports fan interrupted, finishing the last of his beer. Becca looked at the TV and sighed again. She leaned forward and picked up the slacks from the coffee table and made her way back to the bedroom, gently closing the door behind her.

*   *   *

Becca finished the third chant with the girls still staring wide-eyed. She opened her eyes, expecting the light to be different; it wasn't. The girls waited for her to say something, but she didn't. "How do you feel?" inquired Rhonda. "What do you mean?" Becca asked. Rhonda clarified "Do you think it worked?" Becca thought for a moment and replied. "I don't know. I think so, I hope so anyways." Donna tenderly placed her hand on her friend's knee. "If not," she quietly said, "You could always marry Raggedy Andy."

Becca threw Donna's hand off her while Rhonda almost fell off the bed from laughing too hard. "Shut up! Okay, who's next?" said Becca. Donna looked up at Rhonda, still laughing. "Rhonda, you go. I'm still not sure if I buy into all this hooey." Rhonda contained herself with a happy sigh and made her way to the floor with her book and Wal-Mart bag. "Okay, let's see," she said, opening her book. "The Cheaters Spell."

Rhonda pulled the items out of her bag as she listed them off. "One blue candle. One bowl of water. One smooth curved shell," she said as she pulled out a giant conch shell. This time it was Becca's turn to laugh out loud. "What the hell is that?" she squeezed out between snorts. Donna picked the conch up and looked it over. "Yeah. What, is it your turn to speak Piggy?" Becca flew into a fit of hysteria. Donna joined her shortly as Rhonda grabbed the shell away and set it down in front of her.

"It's the only one I could find," she explained. "What was I supposed to do?" Donna wiped a tear from her eye. "Did you ask the Little Mermaid if you could borrow it?" she asked looking back at Becca as the two lost control again, slapping each other on the backs. "It's not the size that matters," Rhonda said, defensively. Becca stopped laughing for a moment to agree, "You know that's true." Rhonda faked a laugh and retorted, "Well, at least I don't look like a dancer from the Nutcracker." Donna doubled over as Becca frowned and glared at Rhonda. Rhonda raised her hands in the air. "Okay, ladies. This is MY room. I am the BOSS in this room, and the boss says shut the hell up or you're both fired," she commanded.

The girls quieted down. "Man, don't piss off the boss," Becca said. "Don't sleep with her either," Donna added. Becca pointed at her friend, "You know, that's also true." "Shut up, damn it!" Rhonda said. "Donna, gimme your lighter." Donna bowed her head and handed it over in subservience. Rhonda swiped it from her and raised an eyebrow. The girls were quiet and composed. It was time for Rhonda to cast her spell. She read from her book.

"Okay, light the candle and take a calming breath. Pour some spring water into the bowl. Hold the seashell in your left hand and wave it over the candle three times. Then place the shell in the bowl of spring water."

The girls watched intently as Rhonda completed each task, until the last one; the giant conch wasn't fitting into the bowl. As she struggled to get the shell to sit without toppling the bowl over, Donna and Becca stifled their laughter, pressing their palms to their lips. Rhonda looked back at the book to make sure it didn't say 'small' shell or 'large' bowl. When she saw it didn't, she went back to her task with full determination. After another moment or two, she laid it just right so the shell was balancing on the edges of the bowl and touching just enough water to satisfy her. She smiled at her accomplishment. "See," she motioned to her friends, "the boss makes it happen." The girls gave a golf clap and she continued. "Now, focus on a beautiful image of the ocean and repeat this chant:

> As the shell remains loyal
> To its ocean home,
> So shall my lovers heart;
> Never will it roam."

Rhonda closed her eyes and repeated the chant again while picturing a beautiful sunset above a crest of waves.

*   *   *

Rhonda stared at the picture on the wall: her and Ben on their honeymoon in Pismo Beach. It had been taken only five years ago. She tried to focus on the happiness she was feeling when she took that picture. She tried to emanate it now within her. After those five short years, there was no happiness left. Ben walked into the bedroom and grabbed his watch off of his dresser.

"Where you going tonight?" she asked her husband. "Out," he answered while fumbling with his watch.

"With who?"

"Brian."

"Where are you guys going to?"

"We haven't decided yet."

"When are you going to be home?"

"Jesus Rhonda, I don't know!" he shouted at her. "Whenever I feel like it. Back off! You're not my warden." He grabbed his wallet and put it in his back pocket.

Rhonda folded her arms across her chest and moved to block the doorway. "No, I'm not your warden," she said. "But I am your wife. Don't you think I deserve a little respect for that, which you can demonstrate by simply telling me what time you're going to be home? You know, in case our children wake up in the middle of the night and want daddy instead of mommy?"

Ben turned to her, staring her down. "Leave me the fuck alone. I'll be home when I decide to come home. Now, shut up and get the hell out of my way." He walked towards the door, lightly pushing her out of his way. She interrupted before he could exit. "Are you going to see *her*?" she asked, not even looking at him, focusing again on the picture on the wall. He stopped in his tracks and stared out into the hallway. "Who?"

Rhonda stayed on the picture, focusing on the sunset in the background. "You know who." Ben turned around and stared at his wife, planting his hands on his hips. "I don't know what the fuck you're talking about." Rhonda could smell the salty air and hear the seagulls flying above. "I found another one of her letters. You don't even try to hide them from me anymore. You obviously love throwing this in my face. I figure we can be honest about it." She turned to face him. Ben rolled his eyes, giving up the charade. "All right, fine. Yes, I'm going to see her."

Even though she already knew, hearing him actually say it hurt more than she expected. Tears welled up behind her eyes. "Do you even love me anymore, Ben?" "What kind of stupid fucking question is that? Of course I love you. I wouldn't be here if I didn't," he said, folding his arms across his chest. She unfolded hers and slowly walked towards him. "But that's the thing, Ben," she said, almost pleadingly. "You're never here. You're always out.....with her."

Ben stepped up to her and pointed his finger at her chest. "Hey! Do you have clothes on your back? Is there food in the fridge? Is there a fucking roof over your head?" Rhonda looked down, a tear escaping from her left eye, falling to her bare feet. It was always this way. "Yes, you have all those things because I provide them for you! And I work hard providing them for you so if I want to go out and have some fun, I'm the fucking man of the house and I'm going to go out and have some fun. Now, mind your own business!"

Ben lowered his hand and turned to leave. "You are my business, damn it," Rhonda said. Ben turned back, pointing his finger right into her face this time. "My business is my business," he said. "Stay the fuck out of it." He lowered his finger and stared her down. She stared back for just a moment, and then lowered her glance downwards. She couldn't hold her tears back any longer. Ben turned back towards the door and started walking through. Rhonda looked up to watch him leave, barely pushing her last words through her lips.

"Ben?" she silently called after him. He stopped in his tracks. Without looking behind him, he shouted. "What!?!" She startled at his volume, and lowered her head again. "Nothing." As Ben headed down the hallway, Rhonda's body shook, and she crumpled to the floor in quiet sobs.

*   *   *

Rhonda chanted a third and final time, and then opened her eyes. "Well?" Becca asked impatiently. "How do you feel?" Rhonda took a moment to think about it. "I don't know," she said, sounding depressed. "You okay, Hon?" asked Donna. "Yeah, yeah I'm fine. I just hope this voodoo works, otherwise I'm going to kill myself." Donna leaned over and put her arm around Rhonda's shoulders. "Oh, please," she said. "You don't think God did a little voodoo back in the day? How else do you think some guys got such big penises and others such small ones?" Rhonda laughed. "What the hell are you talking about?" asked Becca. "I'm just sayin," Donna replied. Rhonda turned her head away for a moment to wipe a small tear from her eye. "Okay, Donna, your turn."

Donna sighed. "I don't know guys. This is super dumb." Becca, still excited, tried to encourage her friend. "Come on, Don, it's only lame if you think it is." "I do think it's lame." "Come on, it'll be fun. We both did it," said Rhonda. Her hopeful friends flanked Donna on either side. She rolled her eyes and slapped her hands onto her thighs. "Alright, alright. Gimme my lighter," she said, grabbing it out of Rhonda's hand. She picked up her little book, turned to the correct page and started reading.

"The Good Luck Love Spell. Red candle, clear vase filled with dirt." Realizing she had forgotten to get dirt, she reached into Becca's bag of soil and grabbed a handful and placed it into the vase in front of her. "Thank you! Okay, package of seeds, a daisy and some water." She then realized she had also forgotten to get water. She motioned towards Rhonda's bottle she had used for her spell. "Hey, gimme that bottle." "Damn Bitch!" exclaimed Rhonda. "You said you had all your shit!" She handed the bottle to Donna. "I lied!" Donna grabbed the bottle from Rhonda and stuck her tongue out at her. Rhonda playfully pretended to grab it.

"Okay," continued Donna. "Light candle. What a surprise. Take a few deep breaths, yada yada yada. Bury all the seeds in the dirt and cover them up. Place the daisy on top of the dirt." As she performed each duty, her annoyance grew more and more. "Now, sprinkle it with water and repeat this chant:

> Planting the seed
> And letting it grow.
> The blossom will bloom,
> My true love will show."

Donna looked to her left. Becca gave her a cheesy smile. She looked to her right as Rhonda gave her a double thumbs-up. Donna looked back at her flowerpot, closed her eyes and repeated the chant again.

*   *   *

Donna looked to her left and then to her right. Nobody else was there in the bar but her and two other guys, one of whom she knew quite well. She took a gulp of her beer. Liquid courage, she thought,

97

you can do this.

While slowly making her way over to them, she pretended to notice the new chairs, the game on the TV, the fact that nobody else was in there. Another gulp of beer down the hatch, and she made her move. "Hey Josh. What's going on?" she asked. "Oh, hey Donna!" said Josh. "I didn't see you there. What a surprise."

Josh and Donna went way back. They had lost touch when they started dating their exes several years ago. Both had just recently split up and after a night of drunken ranting, slept together a week ago. It was something Donna had always thought about. They had a very close bond over the years and he was always there for her, proving his loyalty and faithfulness. She always had a thing for him and thought that maybe now with this experience, they could finally get things going in the right direction for a potential relationship. But she hadn't heard from him since that night and was starting to question any possible romantic future.

Donna smiled, "I'm good, good, thanks. How are you?" He leaned back in his chair and lifted his arms, resting his hands on the back of his head. His confidence was overwhelmingly arousing to her. He replied with a warm grin. "Eh, you know, same ol' same ol'. Hey, let me get you a beer." Josh motioned for the bartender to come over. Donna waved her off. "Oh, no that's okay. I just opened this one." The nerves in her stomach were ready to come out in a big vomitous mess. Josh's friend's cell phone rang. He answered it and headed outside to talk, motioning to the waitress to bring the two guys another round.

Donna was relieved; she did not want an audience for this.

"So how was the rest of your week?" Donna asked after an awkward pause. "Oh, it was fine. Ya know, same shit, different day." Josh seemed nervous. "Well, I never heard from you," she said. "I was hoping......we could....talk.....after...ya know." "Yeah, well," Josh cleared his throat. "Well, it's just that, I....well, I kind of....," he trailed off. Donna looked away. The vomit was beginning to boil in her belly. Josh took a quick breath and stared intently at the label on his beer. "I kind of...got back together with the ex."

There it was. Donna took a drink. "Oh, well," she stammered out, "good for you. I guess."

An hour later, Josh and his friend had gone and Donna was still there alone, getting wasted. She ordered one last beer and a number to a cab company when the stool next to her scooted out, screeching on the polished wooden floor below. Donna looked to see who her fellow commiserator was about to be. As soon as she made eye contact, she wished she hadn't. It was Andy, a once in a while fuck buddy that she hadn't seen since their last encounter. She had almost let herself start to like him when he would call her just to talk, but came to her senses when she realized they really were just friends with benefits.

"Hey Andy! I thought you weren't gonna be in town for like, another two weeks," she slurred at him. "Yeah, that was the plan," Andy said. "But just had some family drama come up so I had to get back into town to deal." Donna tried to act concerned through her inebriated state. "Oh, man, that sucks. Is

everything okay?" Andy ordered a beer and tapped the bar with his knuckles, some invisible rhythm he heard in his mind. "Yeah, you know. The ex is pregnant so we're trying to decide what to do about it." Donna slowly sat straight up in her chair. "Oh my god. How far along is she?" she asked, suddenly beginning to sober up. "Ummmmm, about two months I think," Andy answered. Donna did the math in her head. "That's about the time you were here last," she mentioned. He nodded.
"Yeah."
"With me," she added.
"Yeah it was! Ha! That's hilarious!"
"Isn't it, though."

Andy leaned into Donna's space. The urge to vomit began to rise again.

"You know," he said, "I really enjoyed that. That put a smile on my face for quite a few days." He looked around to confirm confidentiality. "What are you doing after this?" Donna drained her beer and slammed it on the bar. "Taking an AIDS test," she blurted. She grabbed her bag and stood up, giving him one last look. "You dirty bastard," she said, and headed for the door.

She stumbled a little but caught herself against a younger looking douche bag that obviously had a fake ID. "Hey baby! How you doin'?" he asked her. "Oh HELL no!" she replied. She adjusted the shoulder strap on her purse and made her way for the door again, reaching into her pocket for her keys that she'd left on the bar next to Andy.

*   *   *

Donna finished the third chant and kept her eyes closed. She waited to hear magical bells or an explosion, but there was nothing. She opened her eyes, still pointed at her plant. "All right, Skeptic," Rhonda said, "how ya feelin?" Donna shrugged her shoulders. "I don't know. Man, this is so desperate." "It'll work. It has to," said Rhonda. "You don't think it did?" asked Becca. Donna started collecting her items and putting them back in the Wal-Mart bag. "I don't know, Bec. Time will tell, I suppose."

The doubt came off of Donna like steam, unsettling Becca's mood. "What if it doesn't work?" she said, "What if I'm destined to be Robert's housemaid for the rest of my miserable life?" Her girlfriends tried to shush her but she kept going. "What if I never get to walk down the aisle in a beautiful lace gown? I'll never get to experience the amazing joy of motherhood. I'll never get to know what true love is."

"Oh, what the hell is true love anyways?" Rhonda shouted as she stood up from the half-circle. "I got to walk down the aisle in the white gown. I got to experience motherhood. But none of it means shit because I'm with a man that would rather stick his pool cue in another girl's pocket than spend an evening with me and our kids."

Donna intervened. "You guys, calm down." "This is all bullshit. ALL of it," said Rhonda. "The spells. True love. None of it's real." Becca was growing more upset by the minute. "How could it be? I love Robert. I LOVE him. And he doesn't love me enough to make an honest woman out of me. This is just some stupid book written by some stupid fake wannabe witch harping on other women's misery and giving us false hope just so she can make a lousy buck."

"This is bullshit!" shouted Rhonda, throwing her spell book across the room. It knocked over a red glass vase on her dresser, a wedding present from her mother-in-law. Donna and Becca were still. Rhonda's hands shook and she tried to catch her breath.

"Ben will always cheat on me. I will never have it in me to leave him. I will always put up with his lies. He doesn't love me. He never did and he never will." She sat back down on the corner of the bed and started crying.

Becca choked up as well. "I will always settle for Robert. I'm so scared of being alone. Is that so bad? And I'm always going to sew his pants and bring him beer and rub his feet and I'll never get my wedding day in return." She sat next to Rhonda, grabbing her friend's hand and holding it in her own, joining in on the crying.

Donna felt responsible for her friends' despair. She shouldn't have been so cynical about this whole thing. She shouldn't have acted so negatively and been so sarcastic. Being this way had never served her well. Instead, it just bit her in the ass every single time. She had to stop being like this. Living in bitterness came so easily, but it made everything else so much harder to take. It only ever brought her down, and those around her. She had a thought: it was time to change. Donna turned on the ground and faced her friends. "You guys, what if you didn't?"

she asked, placing a hand on both of their ankles. Becca sniffled. "What?"

"What if you didn't settle?" "It's a little too late for that, Don," Rhonda said without looking up. Donna rose to her knees. "It's *never* too late. No matter what we think, there's always time to change." "I'm twenty-six years old, Donna," Becca said. "I don't have much time left. I'm drying up!" Donna emphatically smacked Becca's knee. "Don't be ridiculous! Of course you have time left. How old was your mother when she got married? What, eighteen? No wonder you think you have no time left. You have all the time in the world!"

The girls remained unconvinced and kept sniffling. Donna kept going, determined to break them of this miserable cycle. "Okay, look, what I'm saying is it's never too late to change your life. Who cares if these spells work or not? Who cares if all this is bullshit? We can choose to believe in it, or we can choose to be victims of our own hellish making. I say fuck it. Isn't it worth believing in?" "I believed that Ben would always be faithful to me. You can see how far that got me," said Rhonda. This only made Donna's determination to overcome her cynicism grow stronger. She rose to her feet.

"Okay, so things got fucked up. Big deal, it happens. Things got lost along the way, you were misguided. I mean, who cares if Ben is never faithful to you? Fuck him! There is someone out there smarter and better and more loving than Ben who you deserve and if you believe in that, isn't it possible that you'll find him? And who cares if Robert doesn't ask you to marry him? If he doesn't know that you're the one, then maybe that's your answer. Move on. Find the man of your dreams and marry him. If you believe he's out there, then he is. And who cares if I've made some mistakes recently. A *lot* of mistakes, with some *really* stupid guys. Who cares? If I believe that the one is actually out there, is it really going to hurt me so much? No! If you believe in love, spells or no, it can and will come for you. I cannot live my life being hurt and cynical and leery of every single guy that comes along. I have to believe he is out there, damn it! I have to!"

Rhonda and Becca had stopped crying by the time she finished her speech. They stared up at her, jaws dropped in awe of the normally cynical friend's sudden positive outlook.

"Damn girl," Becca said. "Hit it home." Rhonda nodded, adding, "Sing it from the mountaintop, sister." "I'm serious," Donna sternly said. "We know," said Becca. "We're very impressed."

"Fuck Ben," Rhonda blurted out. "I don't have to put up with this. There would be a lot more money in that jar if I sued his ass for alimony. I don't need him anymore. I don't need *this*." "Fuck Robert," added Becca. "If he can't see how worthy I am of having my dreams come true, of real commitment, then fuck him. He's not worth it anyways." Donna triumphantly raised her arms above her head. "That's what I'm sayin!"

Becca jumped off the bed. "I believe in love!" Rhonda jumped up next. "Me too! I believe in love!" she shouted, with Donna chiming in. The three women laughed out loud at the cheesiness of their statement. Rhonda made her way over to the remnants of the broken vase. She grabbed her little purple book and used it to scrape the shards onto the carpet. The other two laughed again, covering their mouths in disbelief. "What?" Rhonda said, pointing to Becca's pile of dirt. "I gotta vacuum anyways."

She rejoined the trinity in front of her bed and opened her book to the very last page. "Okay, it says here 'To ensure the proper casting of spells, be sure to repeat this final chant four times in order for each element to hear your words.' Man, this is pretty lame." "I'm not saying anything," said Donna. Becca leaned over Rhonda's arm to look at the book. "What's the chant? 'The spell is cast, so let it be.' Easy enough." She bent down and picked up her candle, still flickering, and raised it like a glass of champagne. "Ladies, to love."

Rhonda and Donna reached down to pick up their candles, both still lit. The three witches met their candles in the middle of their small circle and toasted them. "To love!" In unison, they began their chant. "The spell is cast, so let it be." Donna wrapped her arm around Becca's waist. "The spell is cast, so let it be." Becca wrapped her arm around Rhonda's shoulder. "The spell is cast, so let it be." Rhonda looked up at her two friends, and wrapped her arm around Donna's waist. The girls grinned at each other once more. "The spell is cast, so let it be!" All three girls blew out their candles and started cackling as they wrapped their other arms around each other into one unifying embrace, hoping the miracle of love would find each of them sooner rather than later.

Front and back cover photo by Jacob Cadena

-

Front and back cover design by Matt Brewer